Tales from the 2nd Lost Generation

Calgary Writers Montparnasse

CWM

BJT
Calgary

Published by BJT Publishing. Calgary, Canada. First Edition

ISBN: 978-1-7752130-5-5

Forward

Ernest Hemingway's, A Moveable Feast.

It captured my heart decades ago, the idea that burgeoning artists could foster greatness due in part to a strong group bond. Without that coming together of like-minded souls, it's doubtful their individual talents would have soared into the stratosphere as they did, virtually all in later years admitting so.

After retiring full-time from the workforce, I wondered if such a writers group could be found here in Calgary, and after much looking, trial and error, nothing like that unique mix could I locate—of a small, well bonded, hard-working literary group, where the art and trust were paramount, not the personal egos.

By a chance fate and quirky timing, I took over a group and reformed it, making its vision that of the gang from the 1920s Montparnasse scene—Hemingway, F. Scott Fitzgerald, Gertrude Stein, Janet Flanner, Solita Solano, Sylvia Beach, Kay Boyle, and Morley Callaghan, to name a few.

After almost a decade in existence, the Calgary Writers Montparnasse Group is that mix of local artists, serious in their craft, who have a ball when they get together, their egos checked at the door. The genres covered in the CWM are literary, historical, fantasy, mystery, romance, children's, and non-fiction, a mélange of interests from wordsmiths determined to better their craft, one idea, one word at a time... not unlike their beloved Parisian counterparts... cocktails included!

If you like what you see in this anthology and would be interested in joining our gang, email me at:

barbara@booksbybjthompson.com

I have a feeling you'll be glad you did!

Regards,

B. J. Thompson
Organizer, CWM

Table of Contents

Tales from the 2nd Lost Generation

Under the Night Sky

CWM

Dark in the Park

By Iva Polansky

The park paths were designed to offer both a close contact with nature and the open vistas of the city below. Under the night sky, the layout was confusing. Carl had taken his anxiety out for a walk, but now with the hospital out of sight, he was not sure which way led back. His daughter was in there with a post-partum complication and he had a new grandson. The two facts provoked conflicting emotions.

He decided that, right or left, the correct direction was uphill, and headed that way. At the same time, a sharp meow split the air, followed by a series of similar sounds. This was not a cat's wedding, Carl realized. It was a baby, crying. He followed the noise to a lamp-lit bench with a duffel bag posed on top. Inside, he found a newborn child. He stood still for a while, taking in the fact that someone, a mother, did this. Still disbelieving, he turned in all directions looking for human presence. The baby took a pause in crying and he could hear the distant noise from the highway and the light breeze agitating the tree leaves.

Police or the hospital? Hospital, then the police, he decided. He grabbed the bag and set off. There was a swish of bush branches at his side and, in a flash, someone yanked the bag from his grip and started running in the opposite direction. Carl turned on his heels and ran. He was barrelling after a dark-clad, fat hoodie.

Laden as he was with the duffel bag, the kidnapper had no chance. Carl was on him after a few steps and brought him down. Holding him by the neck, face down, he retook possession of the bag.

"That's my daughter," the hoodie said, the voice unmistakably female, almost childlike.

Carl's grip loosened. "Get up," he ordered.

Standing, the girl reached for the bag, but Carl would have none of it.

"That was child abandonment. A criminal offense. It's my duty to report it."

"But I've been here all the time. I've been watching her."

"Why here? Why in the park?"

"It happened here. I mean, the rape. I thought it right to bring the result back here. She was born this morning. No one knows. I didn't know what to do. I just wanted things to get back to normal, you know. Like nothing happened. Like before."
"No one knows? Are you telling me that you were pregnant, and no one noticed?"

"No one. I just looked a little fatter, that's all. I didn't report the rape. I pushed it out of my mind. I liked to pretend it didn't happen. I wanted to pretend nothing happened this morning, too. Then you took her, and I knew it was wrong."

Carl was silent for a while. "Here's what we'll do," he said, at last. "You and I are going to the hospital. You'll check in for a medical exam, you and your baby. After that, you can decide whether you want to keep your daughter, or give her up for adoption. I've got some business at the hospital myself, so I'll keep an eye on you. Let's go."

Tales from the 2nd Lost Generation

The Moonlight No More

By B.J. Thompson

Ice-blue moonlight hues streaked in angular ribbons, seeping through the window sheers, staining the walls and the floor, illuminating the multi shades of grey in Sister Angelica's bedroom, the second hand on her manual alarm clock soft-ticking seconds before midnight.

A bare-wood cross above her black metal bedstead, a small side table, and a narrow wardrobe holding her habit, her black shoes, her Prayer Book and her underclothes were all her worldly goods.

A white cap and plain cotton nightdress covered the Sister's frail body, its neck line high and tied with a simple cotton string. A smaller wooden cross adorned her neck, hanging, it did, from a thin band of smooth brown leather. Sister Angelica had taken to her bed. Mind and body weakness prevented her from fulfilling her religious duties. Prayers and mealtimes she had missed with the other Sisters in the All Saints Cloister.

With a deep but faltering breath, she gave what was left of her strength to raise her hands in a prayer. With her eyes closed, she spoke in a flickering, raspy voice...
Now I lay me down to sleep.
I pray The Lord my soul to keep,
When I die before I wake,
I pray The Lord my soul to take.

A soft grin appeared upon her lips as Sister Angelica's eyes widened, the most they had done in over a week, and the grin becoming a joyous smile, her lips bravely displaying teeth. One more wavering breath in, one final sigh out. Her lungs and her being emptied.

Sister Angelica was no more.
As if in reverence, the moon cast down its bright face saluting her earthly departure, the bleak room cloaked once more in black. The Sister's spirit flew high and wide, seeking, finding, indeed, its holy light-source elsewhere.

Under the Night Sky

By Rob Richards

It wasn't until long after the sun had dipped below the horizon that the glade came to life. The full moon and stars bathed the grass and the trees in a soft silver glow. Figures both miniature, human-sized and giant emerged from the surrounding woods. Some were slender and humanoid, others bestial and misshapen. The moonlight reflected and starlight twinkled in the large, pale but gleaming black eyes of those crouched behind the foliage.

They brought instruments with them; flutes, drums and strange, alien stringed affairs. The largest among them, a furry, horned hunchback, climbed upon an immense stump at the glade's center and put a massive ivory horn to his lips. The sound reverberated throughout the clearing and was carried on the wind to the farthest reaches of the forest. At this signal, spindly, beetle-like creatures formed a circle around him and began playing their own instruments.

Several lithe, elfin dancers pranced, twirled and swayed to the music as the black-eyed creatures watched. The dancers wore flowing, diaphanous robes that glittered with the welcoming light of fireflies which rose in greeting from the underbrush. The music of the beetle men lifted the dancers, tossing them gently in the air and catching them as they drifted back down to earth. The lyrical strains embraced and caressed them and filled their limbs with vigor as the tempo increased. Their dancing became jerky, frenetic. Erratic twists and spins replaced the gentle swaying and twirling.

The fur on the black-eyed ones stood on end, the static in the air crackling through their bodies.

The music came to a halt. The dancers and their audience froze in place and the air in the clearing quivered with anticipation. After a seemingly endless moment, a figure entered the glade. She was nearly as tall as the trees, willowy and clad in a gossamer gown. Her skin was the colour of fresh spring grass, and pale blue blossoms were woven into her hair. A pair of antlers curved upward from her temples. Her milky white gaze met that of the horned one as he stepped down from the tree stump and approached her. The beetle men took up their instruments once more and began to play a low, mournful tune.

The horned one swept the lady of the woods into his arms and the pair glided around the glade in time to the music. The elfin dancers formed a circle around them, swaying and spinning silently as the black-eyed ones looked on in awe. Even the trees moved along to the music, following the lead of the regal pair.

They danced throughout the night under the gentle gaze of the moon. When the first rays of dawn crept above the horizon, the song of the beetle men came to a close without flourish. The black-eyed creatures reacted first. Squealing, they scurried back into the protective darkness of the woods. The elves quickly followed suit, sprinting gracefully back into the trees. The beetle men packed up their instruments, bowed reverently to the lady and the horned one before scuttling into the undergrowth.

Only the lady of the woods and her horned consort remained. They gazed into each other's eyes, then separated as dawn broke. With the sunlight's caress, their bodies began to shimmer and dissolve, and they bowed deeply to one another just before fading entirely.

Under the Night Sky

By L.L. Sheppard

Archer's world tilted, not unlike his stomach, as the lights of the Ferris wheel whirled past in a blur. He couldn't believe he was accidentally seated next to his long-time school crush, Chloe. Inhaling deeply in an effort to restore inner calm, he noted her crisp, summery perfume wafting over him on a gentle breeze infused with the scent of mini doughnuts from the fair grounds. The world tilted again as their cart swung to and fro. He kept his eyes on the starry night sky. Archer didn't chance a look at her, for fear he couldn't tear his eyes away, and she would catch him staring.

At the summit, the cart wobbled to a stop, and Archer felt Chloe's hand grip his arm. Her gulping for air told him she was nervous of heights. All he wanted to do was make her feel safe. Archer shifted slightly in his seat to allow for a furtive glance her way. His eyes locked on hers and he stared into their inky depths. His cheeks flared. Chloe sheepishly looked away, her own cheeks flaring the cutest shade of pink as she removed her hand from his arm. He secretly cursed himself for making her feel uncomfortable.

It took ages for the people at the bottom to disembark which gave him ample time to notice his rapid breathing. Chloe's hand brushed his. Archer wondered if the cart shifted again, but it remained perfectly still. He braved a look at her from under his ball cap. She smiled back at him in a way that made his cheeks feel fire. He reciprocated with a lopsided smile that once appeared would not disappear.

Heart racing and butterflies doing somersaults in his stomach, he took her hand in his and gazed at the stars reflecting in the deep pools of her eyes. Leaning forward, he heard her breath hitch. She leaned in, and their lips met.

Their world stopped... and started anew as the Ferris wheel made its slow decent to the ground.

Chloe sat back in her seat, smiling. "I can't believe how long I've wanted to do that!" she exclaimed with a giggle. Archer couldn't believe his ears. "Y-you have?" he stuttered, unsure if he had heard her correctly.

"Of course!" she said, as she leaned in and kissed him on the cheek, "I'd really love to go out sometime," she chirped.

He shot her a grin normally found only on a boy on Christmas morning.

"I'd love that!" he blurted out, as they both began to laugh.

The teens exited the Ferris wheel and parted ways back to their own group of friends, promising to make plans for a real date when they saw each other at school the next day. Archer walked out into the nearly empty parking lot where his dad was supposed to pick him up and flopped down on the curb to wait. He drew in his knees and lowered his head in shock. *I can't believe she kissed me,* shaking his head in utter amazement. *What a night!*

Ring of Darkness

By William Alan Gardner

Organy pushed softly along a trail that wound through trees. They were mostly spruce with the occasional aspen and birch, common trees in this part of the forest. It was starting to snow with large soft flakes floating down from a dull sullen sky. Already there were several centimeters on the trail, laying down a light blanket that muffled sound. The silence sharpened his hearing, adding an edge to his already heightened senses. He was moving quickly on the unfamiliar trail so didn't see the clearing until he came over a rocky rise and there it was spread out below. He stopped quickly, crouching down while his eyes darted over a sight that was utterly discordant this deep in the forest. Within the silence he could hear his heart beating just that much faster.

A ring of large vertical stones capped by other stone lintels made a circle in the center of the clearing. The lintels were smooth polished and the outer side was decorated with carved symbols or runes. The lack of shadow made it difficult to see them clearly. Whatever the origin, they were unfamiliar to him. From his vantage point he was about level with the capstones and noticed that there appeared to be a haze between the columns that made it difficult to see into the center.

Organy waited for five minutes, Ten. Then, with no indication of danger, his curiosity took over and he made his way down the slope into the valley clearing. The clearing itself was flat and perhaps a hundred paces from side to side with the stone ring right in the center. He made almost no sound in the falling snow as he approached the ring, circling it entirely and slowly. Unconsciously he counted the columns. There were thirteen in all, each about an arm's length on a side, and with a space of about three arm lengths between each one. He stopped and then stepped up to one of the gaps, extending his arm into the shimmering haze and finding nothing. His arm simply went through and then could be withdrawn easily. After a few moments of uncertainty he walked up to and through the haze, coming out on the inside of the stone ring and into warmth and bright clear moonlight. The change from cold and light snow startled him but not as much as the woman standing by a raised pool in the center of the right. She turned and looked at him, beckoning for him to come closer. "I've been *waiting," she said. Her voice was soft and clear as if bypassing his ears and echoing directly in his brain.*

Within this strange stone ring he felt different, divided, as if his natural cautionary instinct was somewhere else. Lost. Organy blinked, adjusting his cloak and loosening the mithcutler hanging from his left shoulder. He felt confused yet somehow knew he had a connection to this person, had known her in a dim past, and that he would do whatever she asked. He dropped the mithcutler on the ground and walked slowly toward her. She took his hand, bringing him to the edge of the stone-crafted raised pool of clear still water.

"I think I know you," he stammered.

"Yes," she said. "I am Talisha. You know me as I know you. Come, look into the water and tell me what you see. Do not be afraid."

Looking at her for reassurance, Organy bent over the pool and looked into the water, wanting yet not wanting to see anything. He had heard about the perils of scrying. At first there was just the water with the bright reflected moonlight. Then as he looked deeper he saw what he had hoped he would never have to see. He struggled backward with a cry, turning and running toward one of the gaps in the ring of stones but, as he approached it, a vision of a tall woman with the face of death stood there holding out her hand in a gesture of 'stop'. As he turned toward other gaps the same vision was there, each one blocked. Behind him he heard Talisha say softly "You cannot leave this place. Not yet."

My One Bad Night

A Night to Remember

By William A. Gardner

The gun in her hand was black. The dim bus lights bounced off brushed steel.

Looking up I recognized the dress first, a yellow floral print that fell below the knees over a set of black Lululemon yoga pants, and below that a pair of orange sneakers. But it didn't click until I saw the eyes. Even with the mask I could still see the eyes clearly - green with orange flecks. She lived in an old two-story clapboard house next to mine.

As in so many neighbourhoods the builders had saved design money by printing two mirror-image plans for adjacent houses. This layout placed her bedroom window directly opposite mine. With narrow lots her bedroom window was no more than ten feet away. She had this habit of not closing her curtains and walking around her room wearing skimpy lingerie or 'nothing but a smile' as the song says. I would stand in my own bedroom with the lights out and watch her through half-closed curtains with a morbid fascination.

The conflict between fascination, arousal and guilt plagued me until the time I caught her standing at the window staring directly at me. I was frozen in place with the taste of guilt in my mouth, even though I was sure that she couldn't see into my darkened room. *Did she know?*

It struck me then that she was showing off, projecting her sexual power, daring me to reveal myself. Oh, the naked female body with its curves and dark places—it was surely an invitation to dominate or submit. Men have the power of size and strength; women, the power of sexual attraction. She certainly knew how to use hers.

We had been neighbours for about six months. Typical in a modern suburban way we almost never spoke, just a nod or restrained wave. The only time we exchanged more than a word was once when she knocked on the door and asked to borrow ten dollars for something - I can't even remember for what - saying that she was a little short that month.

"Sheila," she had said with a slight smile when I asked for her name. No last name, just Sheila. I had handed her the ten spot and she walked away leaving me with a dumb look on my face. She had never paid it back and I was too awkward to ask. Perhaps she felt that I was getting my money's worth by watching her. She was older than I, although probably not by much. She had a pretty face that also suggested a life of hard knocks. There was something in her eyes that suggested fear and defiance. Now on the bus I had a choice to make, and it could be worth my life.

She worked her way down the aisle of the bus, waving the gun and getting people to drop cash, watches and other jewelry into a Superstore bag. She had climbed onto the bus behind a few others. Clever. It was the last day of the month when many had just cashed their paycheque and were heading home to enjoy an evening with the family or perhaps a dinner out and movie. As the bus started off she told the driver to keep driving then fired a pistol shot through the ceiling to get people's attention and let them know she was serious. People definitely took her seriously.

One fella a few rows up objected so she pistol-whipped him and then put the pistol to his ear. He didn't even bother to pull the cash out of his wallet but just dumped the whole thing quickly into her bag. Now she looked at me as I got the cash out of my pocket. I averted my eyes,

looking down. She must recognize me I thought, but if she realizes that I recognize her then she'll likely put a bullet in my head. I kept my head down, trying desperately to not look at the eyes behind the mask. I dropped the cash into her bag.
"Is that all?" she demanded, daring me to look at her. I took off my watch and added it to the loot, noticing the clunk as it landed on other watches. *Shit, I liked that watch.*

"Cellphone!"

I dragged it out and dropped it into the bag but that made me angry. She hadn't taken any other phones. That thing was my life. *Fuck it.* I looked up directly into her eyes, defiant, saying nothing. She stood there, staring at me, daring me at gunpoint. The moment seemed to stretch into infinity, and then she moved on. I thought that I could hear a slight 'hah' from under the mask. Then she shouted for the driver to stop and was gone out the back door.
That night, before bed, she stood again at the window, facing me, running a hand over her bare, taut skin. In her other hand she displayed a cellphone and stared across the inky void that divided us.

I watched. The Universe waited, silent.

Then I went downstairs and retrieved two beers from the fridge. Once outside, I pushed through the dividing hedge, mounted her front step and knocked on the door.

50 Shades of Red

By Iva Polansky

The day Paul Anderson was disinherited started with his mother's phone call.

"Today's the day," she said. "The books are at the post office and Rob will pick them up in the afternoon. Lizzie's ordered fifty copies for the crowd. And–just imagine! –Grandma was released from the hospital yesterday. She insists on attending the event."

Cousin Lizzie was definitely moving up the town's cultural ladder. Paul remembered her as a dizzy blonde, whose reading matter was limited to glossy magazines. When he heard that she took over the town's only bookshop, he thought the task was beyond her. Still, it was wrong to judge her without a try. His own book, The Helping Hands, a memoir of his volunteer job in Papua New Guinea, had just been published. When Mother suggested a promotional event at Lizzie's bookshop opening, as a gesture of family solidarity, he was willing.

"Lizzie will take care of everything," Ma said. "She'll order the books and send out invitations. All you have to do is show up, read a chapter, and sign the copies."

Paul was nervous. This was his first signing event, his first public appearance, and that it would happen in front of former schoolmates, who knew him as the local nerd did not help the matter. Yet he was a winner after all. He had something to show to the former bullies. He had seen the world, taught classes in a tropical forest, survived in tough conditions, and had written a book about it.

The car accident happened four blocks away from the bookstore. It was his fault. Nothing serious, just a scratch, but he had to wait for the police. He was already late due a rainstorm and the ensuing bumper-to-bumper traffic. His cell clamoured for attention.

where the hell r u? Cousin Rob texted.
liz frantic everybody waiting

Traffic accident. Tell her to start reading
I'll sign after

ud better

Cousin Rob, Lizzie's brother, had large muscles and small patience for nerds. Paul began to sweat when the next message came in fifteen minutes later, Granny sez ur disinheruted I say ur dead.

When he finally reached the bookstore, it was deserted.

"Where's everyone?" he asked the weeping Lizzie, sitting hunched over a table laden with untouched egg salad sandwiches, cheese cubes, and crackers.

"Go away," she yelled. "You've ruined me!"

Her mother, refusing to look at Paul, began packing away the food, and said, "They're all gone. You didn't say you wrote pornography. You should've warned us. Grandmother was shocked. Everybody was."

Paul swallowed, "Pornography?" He reached for a book from the pile, My Teasing Hands by P. H. Anderson. "That's not my book. Mine's called The Helping Hands. And my middle name is Anthony."

"I accidentally deleted your email with the title," Lizzie said, wiping her eyes. "I remembered that it had something to do with hands."

As it turned out, Lizzie was wrong about being ruined. In a town where a best-selling title sold at the most five copies, her entire stock of My Teasing Hands disappeared within a week of the book's release.

A Quietus Peace

By B.J. Thompson

The entire week had been magical.

Upscale dinner parties, photo shoots, press conferences and interviews, then the raison d'être—the awards ceremony. I had never experienced such a formal event, and at the Oslo City Hall to see men attired in coattails and women in Dior gowns and evening gloves, well, it was a Cinderella dream come true, not celebrating mere beauty but brilliance. The Chairman of the Norwegian Nobel Committee walked up to the microphone and called my name;

> Barbara Joan Thompson, Canada, for her work, entitled, Beyond the Realm of Possibilities, the Nobel Peace Prize for Literature, 2020

I rose from the Queen Anne chair, clasped in my gloved hands the folds of my ivory Moiré taffeta gown, and carefully took the stage. In front of the King of Norway, the Chairman opened the velvet box and extracted the

medallion, the solid gold metal shimmered in the blinding klieg lights.
A slip of my gloves along its silken surface had the disc fly from his fingers and into the air, its weight allowing for increasing speed. As deadly in flight as a Japanese shuriken star, the medal sliced over the shocked crowd, its destination: that of the neck of a security guard standing in the shadows. The heavy disc dove hard and deeply lodged like a logger's axe-head into the man's carotid artery, blood ejecting as if pressurized water from a hellish fireman's hose.

In a panic, the guard reached to free himself from the assault, and his hand inadvertently hit the panic button affixed to the call switch of his inner ear radio, the silent alarm sending out a Code Red terrorist intruder alert. Guards with AK 15s, 47s, and fully auto Glocks swarmed all entrance points, the honoured guests and recipients yelling, shrieking, aghast at the nightmarish sight. All sprang from their chairs, still holding the evening's silver programme cards, the metallic gun-metal grey velum paper glinting in the light, giving the illusion of handguns.
In a closing circular attack stance, every guard raised arms and fired; the blast of air, the smell of gun powder, the cries, and then the silence. Within minutes, every

attendee became a recipient of metal ore all their own, though far less precious, their bloodied and lifeless bodies impaled by full metal jacket bullets, evisceration and annihilation at every turn.

Nay but one. Me.

Shell-shocked and stunned, I staggered to the microphone, cleared my constricted throat, and stammered,

Thank you, uh, ever so much for this generous... award. Justification that hard work pays, affirmation that all things are indeed possible. Um... thank you.

I wiped the blood splatter from my blushing cheeks and tip-toed off the stage and over bodies as I exited the hall. In passing, I knelt down and daintily dislodged my medallion from the blood-soaked neck of the dead guard. Reaction: It's nice to travel, but it's always good to get home.

Canada. My Cave. My Rock.
A Noble kind of Peace.
It and I shall remain.

Journal Entry from the Perspective of Your Favourite Animal

The Squirrel Diaries

By L.L. Sheppard

Nut date: Sept 29th

Dear Diary,

Egads! It's so cold out! The first day of autumn has come and gone and I find myself trying to forage for food; however, the pickings are slim. Steve the raven came flying around my tree earlier this morning, caw-cawing as usual about "doomsday" and "winter is nigh," but, of course, he's like this every year when the days turn cooler and the leaves start to fall. I suppose he does have a point. I was shivering when I woke up and had to pull the leaves right up under my chin.

I so did not want to get up!

That reminds me... I saw the prettiest leaf at lunch today. It was all splotched with reds, oranges and yellows; all the fall colors in one tiny leaf! Can you imagine? I brought it home with me and I might give it to Hazel as a best friend present. I just know she will love it and keep it all winter! She gets me an acorn every year and this year I

want to give her something really special because it's her third winter coming up.
Side note: my tail is NOT getting any bushier... and it's supposed to. I've been waiting to show it off, but it's still so scraggly. I guess my winter coat still has to come in and it's only the beginning of fall, but I find myself impatient. Chloe told me today that maybe in a month it would start to look fluffier, but she's a goose—what the heck does she know?

Tonight is the annual Autumn Ball and I sure hope Nutters asks me to dance! He is so fluffy and handsome. The old and wise squirrel, Scruzzlesnout, says he will be making a big announcement. I am excited to hear what he has to say as I'm sure it's about the coming cold. There will be lots of critters about to chat with and discuss the news. It's so nice to have a fun goodbye for the birds who fly south and to end the summer with a bang. I suppose I should go preen my fur for the big event. I'll tell you all about it tomorrow, dear diary. Wish me luck!

Sincerely,
Luna the squirrel

Mission: ImPussyable

By B.J. Thompson

Tale begins with the Mission Impossible Theme Song. Substitute the musical sound "da" for "meow."

0500: There's the sound I've been waiting for! It's Fat Cat outside in the alley, howling us to muster. Today is Torment Thursday and we're all ready to rummblllle!

My name is Tiger, yes, Tiger, aka, Teeny Tiger, aka Tiger-Puppy, aka Teeny-Tiger-Puppy-Face; although, I am not a tiger nor a puppy. I am a cat. I live with my two bratty cat sisters, Matty, aka Matty-bear, aka Killer, and Kaley, aka, Kaley Cupcake, aka Kaley Kit Kat, aka Pudgy.

As soon as the howling siren is heard, we jump from our Tiger, Kaley and Matty beds and bound upstairs to Grandma's bedroom–the key to our freedom lies within her grasp, for she is the morning gatekeeper. We jump on her, purr up her nose, lick her face, rattle her closet doors, cry incessantly and claw her walls with a kind of nails-onblackboard effect, full-on and without end until she can take no more, and with a kind of grumbling ferocity rises from her stead to open the patio door.

Matty sedately strolls with confidence and Kaley is fat and slow, so I leap over both of them like a frolicking fawn… WHEEEE, I go, clean through the air, light as a feather. I'm adorable but I'm small. Still, I'm the furry man of the house and don't you forget it!

The wailing doesn't stop from Fat Cat until all are assembled at the Muster Point: The Big Bush on the Green Space, we've made a kind of furry fort back there, all stealthy-like.

"Okay, Pussy Posse, gather 'round," barks out Fat Cat, the bravado, stance and voice of a feline General Patton, carrying with great panache a tree twig as a baton, "today is Torment Thursday, our neighbourhood patrolling done for the week, our birdie and mousy catch quotas filled, our haranguing the squirrels a 'fait accompli,'" says our pussy Patriarch of 58 Back Street Alley. He is white with gray patches and the size of a furry Marlon Brando… when Marlon preferred ice cream over women.

All of us nod in the affirmative, jubilant, with toothy smiles and bugged-out eyes, paws punching the air, and high-fours all around. Fat Cat's little brother, Baby-boy, and Matty-bear, Kaley Cupcake, Terrence Tabby, and Bob Black Cat make up our gang... and me, of course, the runt, ever joyful but not so bright they tell me, but dead adorable, of that there is no doubt.

0530: Mission: Two doors down, make that dirt ball of a dust-bunny dog, Tommy Terrier, lose the plot.

0600: One by one, we jump, ever stealthy, with cat-burglar-like precision, to perch on top of Tommy's fence—four at the corners and three on the sides. In turns, we mock this hairy hound. Tommy Terrier jumps and jumps and barks and barks, rounding his yard in each direction, leaping with all his might, never coming close to his prey. We smile, we flip-top-head yowl in delight, we put our paws behind our ears and stick out our pink tongues, caterwauling in kitty lingo, "Na, Na, Na-Na, Naaa!" the mutt whirling into a freaky frenzy of frustration and drooling froth.

0630: Tommy Terrier collapses onto the yard, upside down, eyes rolled back, tongue dangling. His master, confounded, carries him inside and we yowl with glee. Mission Complete.

A Page from the Cat's Diary

By Iva Polansky

They called in the dog psychologist, which means that Precious is in real trouble. I must confess that I am exhausted because it took a lot of effort to get things up to this promising point.

The psychologist wanted us in the same room to see how we two interact. Seeing me, Precious started to convulse and whimper. I acted terrified and sought the protection of my Mom's lap. The psychiatrist wrongly concluded that Precious was about to attack me. As if.

Personally, I have nothing against Precious. He is already suffering from abuse by his owner. To be a Bichon Frisé is bad enough. To be a Bichon Frisé dyed pink and wearing Zirconia studs in the ears must be hell. My aim is not to drive Precious mad. I only want his owner to pack her bags and leave Mom and me alone. Like in the good old days.

The psychologist inspected my litter box to assess Precious's criminal activity. As usual, it was in a terrible state, with half of the kitty litter scattered about. Also, Precious's paws were embedded with some litter and my poop. Since he is a stupid dog, he can't lick them clean, and he isn't smart enough to avoid my litter box when I'm chasing him. The psychologist left. My Mom and her girlfriend are conferring in private. If the litter box scheme doesn't work, I will be forced to escalate the situation by doing my business on the girlfriend's clothes. I know from experience that the stink needs three consecutive laundering's before the clothes can be worn again.

And now I'm forced to put aside my domestic affairs and obey my natural instinct. Two pigeons have landed on the patio. I feel a pressing need to catch them.

The Myth of the Wind

By Christianne Parrott

The myth of the wind
Came up now and then,
On the forest floor.
The mice would pretend,
They could hear the wind
Telling its tales,
Of gusts and gales
And journeys without end.

But alas there was no wind
On the forest floor,
Nowhere to be found,
They could feel it no more.
The wind was a myth,
Downgraded to lore.

It had never been seen.
It had never been heard.

Not even the elders of

Elders could say
That the wind did exist,
A fact and not myth. But the birds would insist
That the wind was around,
A real thing they said,
That even made sound.

The mice knew better

Than to believe in tall tales,
Not one mouse had ever
Felt the wind on their tail.
How could these birds
Think the mice so naïve?
The wind was a fable,
They could never believe.

The trees of the forest

Were dense and lush,
They felt safe down low
Deep in the brush.

Safe in the warm
And quiet and known.
They felt no need
To question or roam.
No desire to see
Or even be shown.

And the wind was forgotten
A myth no more.

My Walk on the Beach Ended with the Discovery of a Severed Foot

CWM

Dancing on the Beach

By William Alan Gardner

"No, no, no, no" she said emphatically. "I will not stay here. I want to go out, to play. Can we go to the seashore? Please!" Her voice was pleading but her face had that determined look.

"But it's getting late, it will be dark soon," her father said. "Perhaps another time... tomorrow, maybe."

He looked the dark circles around the eyes, her expression of hope and expectation. Her thin blonde hair tumbled around her drawn face, the golden hue contrasting with her dark brown eyes.

"But I really want to go now."
"Are you sure? It could be dangerous."
"Yes, daddy, I'm sure. I want to go now."
"Well, alright. If we hurry we could catch the sunset."

He helped her dress and together they went down to the car. It was an old Volkswagen bug that he had driven since his hippy days, green with a few small stick-on flowers still evident on the rear driver side. He was the kind of person that didn't get rid of things just because they were out of date. "If it's not broke don't try to fix it," he'd say. His friends would kid him about it but he didn't really care. That habit left him with some extra money that he had regularly put away for Katrina's education. She was all he really cared about.

They drove around the bay to the East side. The beach there was mostly rocky with a few sandy patches. Nearby was the trendy coffee shop where he'd met Katrina's mother. It was a good place to watch the sun slide below the horizon. He parked and they got out. Taking her hand they walked along the beach. He didn't want to let go of her hand but she pulled it away and ran out to the rocks with him tagging along.

"I want to dance," she said, determined to cheer herself up. "I might as well make some use out of those lessons."

She jumped up on one of the larger rocks and started to dance, flinging her hands up and around, her feet pumping and her hair flying out in all directions, her small feet jumping in yellow running shoes. She danced to celebrate life, her life.

The father's phone suddenly sprang into a musical ringtone.

"Hello," he said. "Yes, we just came from there. Kat wanted to visit the beach. I couldn't say no. She's dancing on the rocks. We'll head back to the hospital later after stopping for a snack. You know how she loves pizza. Yes, I know."

He turned is head to watch his daughter who, now out of breath, sat on the rock. She was looking west, watching as the yellow orb sank below the water. The fading light caught in her wind-blown hair creating a halo effect. *She looks happy.* Then he turned away and walked a few steps up the beach, passing an old running shoe lodged between two rocks.

"No, he said softly into the phone," his breath catching in his throat. "Not long, not long now."

Getting Lucky

By Christianne Parrott

He was definitely getting lucky tonight.

Everything was perfect. The night breeze was warm, wafting over the ocean into the tranquil bay where they walked. Cicadas hummed the background to a choir of frogs, birds, waves and sweet late-night silence. The moon was low and full over the water, casting a rippling reflection.

The whole evening had, for once, gone his way. Their dinner was excellent, and in this part of the world he never had to worry about the bill. She didn't seem phased with his almost unwavering interest in her breasts, and she actually laughed at his jokes. She made no secret of her increasing infatuation as they danced at the nearby beach bar.

She walked by the water's edge, saying nothing, her body language screaming at him to throw her into the sand and take her right there. He knew from experience that sex on the beach was a far better fantasy than reality, and though it took some force of will, he remained patient.

He was sure of foot and strode beside her with all the confidence of a known outcome.

~~~

She was definitely getting lucky tonight.

Her anticipation increased with every step. Unbelievably, her luck had turned. The whole night had gone off without a hitch.

Unlike wobbly heels on a slick floor, dancing barefoot on the beach came natural. Falling on sand held no danger of a broken limb. The beach seemed like the perfect place to have their inevitable 'romantic interlude.' Yet, unbeknownst to her, sand had a way of ruining a good time between lovers.

Her patience gone, she grabbed his hand and twirled into him, her intention to sweep him off of his feet and into her sarong. Being caught off guard, he stumbled in the momentum, and the pair became a spiralling mass of tangled limbs flailing at all angles as they collapsed into the soft sand.
~~~

A howl erupted as her knee punched his groin. He rolled away, elbowing her chin. He froze when his back collided with something solid, yet squishy. Jerking up, he reached for the offending object, and for a split second his brain told him he had grabbed his date by the leg. Reason overtook as he dropped the severed limb and screamed into the night.

Nobody was getting lucky tonight.

Two Dismembered Feet

By B. J. Thompson

I'd walked that beach so often.

I knew every pebble and every grain of sand. Over and over, and over again, starting here, getting there. Every time.

I walked this beach, that way, because I knew no other.

Today, miles along, out of breath and out of patience, I trudge and then I stop. I don't usually stop at this point. Something made me stop.

I look down. Below me lay two dismembered feet.

I look to my left and to my right. Nothing else and no one. The beach held only me. The waves lapped in, soft and slow. High Tide was nigh.

Then a voice...

I allowed you to walk on your own, your way. Years and years washed by as you walked, getting nowhere, and I

watched. I shall not allow you to walk another foot until you choose the right path and walk with conviction.
I look down, and I see legs cut off at the ankles. I giggle, as they remind me of two Captain Hook legs. My eyes explode and all circulation arrests in my brain when I realize those legs are mine.

And those feet are my feet!

Lying on their sides, left and right, splayed out, as if unceremoniously chopped off and dropped. Yes, I'd recognize those feet anywhere. There was no blood. Odd, that.

I keel over into the sand, standing only as long as I thought I had support. Funny thing: How did I manage that?

Man can do miraculous things without my help, Barbara. Man can also do destructive things, especially to himself. Walk in ways that are not proper, not meaningful, not befitting the life I gave. You do not appreciate my gift? I will remove your ability to go forward until such time as you do.

I sat there; the waves sploshing in and around my outstretched Captain Hook legs. The tide, coming closer,

I feared drowning. I'd never been without feet. How, now, do I escape what I fear?

And, how do I regain what I purposely squandered?

I bowed my head and cried. My hands balled into fists, my thumbs crooked, hiding within my palms. I felt as a little girl... so afraid. I knew I had no right to ask for a second chance. But silently, unknowingly I guess, I did ask, and He listened.

That day, I was carried off the beach by Him because on that day, as in all the days before, I had no appreciation.

On the days to follow, I will choose to walk the way of the righteous, and earn back His gift of walking at all.

To fall, and be carried away, that's divine help; more so, an earthly lesson learned.

The Fountain of Youth Bakery

The Fountain of Youth Bakery

By L. L. Sheppard

It's a long and lonely road that a vampire walks.

Nothing and no one lasts. Throughout the ages, it's you and not another living soul sharing your long existence. Except for other vampires like me...

"This is what you are choosing—death—but not your own? The death of everyone you once knew and cared for... is this what you want? For all eternity? You keep living, meeting people, just for them to die?"

He nods, thinking he understands, but no one can truly understand the crippling loneliness that is my existence. I am trying not to sway his decision to merely end my own suffering.
"Are you sure you want to be... like this?"

I wave my arm across my torso, outlining my dark countenance. A bit over dramatic, but then, who am I if not an entertainer? Tearful doe eyes, pleading eyes, beg up at me in the darkness, and barely audible, even to my superior hearing, is the exhale of a whispering,
"Yes."

Then with more conviction, "I love you. For God's sake, Ravenna. Yes."

I hesitate—feel the deep red subcutaneous liquid calling to me. I smell it, metallic, sweet, beckoning me to indulge, and in so doing, turning another into a nightmarish creature. I hold my breath to avoid inhaling any more of the fragrance. I fast lose dominion over my hunger. My fangs begin their descent, and I salivate. This is it, the end of my control. I will feed and he will turn. Decision time is over. I am ravenous. I thrust my wrist out at him, "Eat. Now." *He grabs my hand, pushing the cherry pie into his eager lips.*

"Mmpft..."

He mumbles as he devours with all speed the whole piece, no choking. The confectionary hits his stomach and his eyes roll back, his face slackening. His body heaves onto the floor and shudders before seeing anew. His vampire eyes look around, seeing things once they could not see. The detail... so great. It is painful. They lock onto mine.

"I... I had no idea this bakery existed until tonight. What have I done?"
He cradles his head.

"Hush now," I coo, "it's okay, my love. We can be together forever now, eating as much of this cherry pie as we wish. This is our fountain of youth."

Calming now, he gazes upward, and a devilish smile surfaces.

"In that case, I'll have another slice."

Confession of a Former Woman

By Iva Polansky

My husband left me because of an older woman.

She did not seduce him. She hardly knew him and he hardly knew her, yet he left me because of her. It was thanks to her and her secret recipe that I lost my menses along with my pubic hair, and my breasts shrank to their pre-pubescent nothingness. Francis said he was sorry, but he felt like a pedophile while making love to me. He just couldn't take it. I don't blame him, how could I? I blame her, Susan, the baker.

Also, I blame the other victims who chose to stand behind Susan. They wouldn't sue her for what they called an understandable error. They said that she was so deeply distraught by the fire in her kitchen that she was unaware she doubled the key ingredient in the pie filling. They accepted her apology.

Herbert Crow, whose fifty-year-old body now has the look and energy of a teenager's, got hostile to the point of threatening me with bodily harm if I dared contact a lawyer. He said Susan's mistake was a blessing. He could finish high school and do something meaningful with his life—maybe even go to university—instead of working as a watchman in a meat plant.

The others, too, tried to talk me out of suing. They argued that ever since Susan opened her bakery, there were no longer any age-related ailments in our community; no Alzheimer's, no loss of sight or hearing, and no arthritis pain.

Even the bone density tests kept coming back with robust numbers. They were sorry for my loss, they said, but I should keep quiet for the common good. Jennifer Brandt murmured that had I not devoured the whole pie, I wouldn't be in this predicament in the first place. I heard that clearly.

I do hate them. I hate the whole bunch of the insensitive, selfish creatures. They told me that I'd grow out of it. That in a few years, I'd be an adult once more. That I'd find another man, maybe even a better one, who would stick with me no matter, unlike Francis. They didn't understand. They were not with me at night when I howled in despair. They were not with me in that cold bed. I wished them all in hell; Susan, Herb, Jennifer, and the rest, and I was not patient enough to wait for God to arrange the transfer. After all, my hell was here and now.

So I did it. In the dark of night, I set the bakery on fire. I watched the bright flames consume the building with both Susan and her secret recipe inside. After all, this was what was done to sorceresses in the Middle Ages, when people acted in good faith.

I now sleep in a single prison cot. It isn't a comfortable arrangement, but I no longer feel desperately unhappy. When I get my freedom back, I'll again be a woman.

Monterey Pop Pie

By B. J. Thompson

At ten minutes passed the witching hour of October 4, 1970 these words were spoken...

"Peggy, give me a hit, man. The session was good, but tough, I gotta come down."

"No. You're clean. Don't fuck it up."

"Listen, I know where you got it and who you got it from. I can do the same thing you did."

"Then do it. It's not coming from me."

Slam went the door of room #103 at the Landmark Hotel, Hollywood. Minutes later, bang went the back passenger door of a limo, its tires squealing onto Franklin Avenue, the black beast headed for the corner of North Sycamore and Hollywood Boulevard. The land-yacht parked just shy of the intersection, the passenger forced to get out and walk. There could be no overt meeting, no

limos, no celebrity scene of any kind, if the deal was to go down.
Feet from the bougainvillea bushes and wild ivy where the dealer stood, pacing back and forth, jonesin' himself for a fix, a marketer's cart was parked on the sidewalk, a pleasant-looking obstacle situated between reality and chemical escape.

Stopping in her tracks, as she wasn't in a complete hurry, the bubbly chick lowered her rose-coloured glasses, and said, "Hey, man, what you sellin'?"

The marketer, sporting a white cap and a blue and white striped apron, looked up, smiled, and said, "Pies, miss, I sell pies."

A flip-top head laugh, then she asked, "Here, man, you sell pies here? You get a lot of pie biz on the Boulevard?"

"Many people who get high, ponder pie, yes. I do a decent biz. Would you like one of my pies to take home with you?"

"Oh, hey, I ain't out here for no pie, man. I'm here for another treat," laughing, winking, with a childlike smile. The rock star thought for a moment, then said, "Hey, do you have peach pies? My Mom used to make a mean one back in Port Arthur. I miss my Mom."

"I'm fresh out of peach, but I do have this lovely cream pie; fresh coconut, real whipped cream, with a dash of Eternal Youth spice."

"Eternal youth!" said the 27-year-old woman, a big belly laugh this time, her long, wild hair flicking, her beaded necklaces jangling, all from accentuated movement, always hyper she was.

She asked, "That pie got a name? Is it popular?"

"Monterey Pop Pie. I only offer it to special customers."

"Oh, like who? Anybody I'd know?"

"Well, recently, Rudy Lewis from The Drifters and Frankie Lymon from The Teenagers."

"Hey, they're all musicians, man, and they copped it from heroin OD."

"Yes, that's correct."
"So, your eternal youth pie didn't work. It ain't worth shit."

"Oh, it would have worked, had they accepted my offer. So, can I tempt you?"

"Uh, no way, man, why do I want to be young forever? I've lived a thousand lifetimes already."

"Suit yourself," shrugging his shoulders, throwing a wink to the amused but confused woman, who bedecked in tie-dye, looking like the inside of a psychedelic kaleidoscope, sauntered down the street in search of her dealer.

The marketer drew down the blinds on his stall, the cart rhythmically squeaking as it rolled out of sight.

Two hours later...

"Hey, what's with all the lights and sirens?" said a man, dressed in a white cap and striped apron, standing on the sidewalk at 7047 Franklin.

"Overdose, groupies sayin'. Some say it's room 105. That's where she was stayin', man."

"Dead?"

"Yeah, Janis."

"Hey, kid, you a rocker?

"Yeah, my name's Brian, man, Brian Cole, from the band, The Association. Me and my guys just got back from a gig up at Monterey."

"Do you feel like a piece of pie?"

Mother Shipley's Pie Shop

By William Alan Gardner

My Grannie never seemed to age. Oh, some days she looked rather frayed at the edges the way you'd expect old people to look. Other days she seemed like her old self, full of enthusiasm and laughter and hardly a wrinkle except for her laugh lines and an old scar below her left eye. She was a great cook and had a pastry shop on Ponce de Leon where she sold all manner of pastries, croissants, pies and other confections. After school my sister and I would head over to her shop and try to surprise Grannie by sneaking in the back door. That was another strange thing about her. She always seemed to know things like forecasting the weather, if we misbehaved school, and when we were going to show up for some pastries and a story.

Yes, stories. She had stories about the history of St. Augustine, about people in old England or France, and even about pirates and buccaneers. The stories seemed so real and told in such detail, it was as if she was reliving them in her memory. Well, after a cheese croissant and perhaps a chocolate wheel or some other delectable we would plead with her for another story. If she wasn't too busy, she would sit in the rocking chair, the one in the kitchen corner by the stove, arrange her apron properly - she was a very proper lady - fix us with an intent look, and start in a low monotone;

"Now here's a tale to make you shake, and on its truth my honor stake. Long choices made and evil crossed, knowledge gained and wisdom lost. So keep the faith and ring the bell, hold thy tongue and listen well."

Then she would ring a little bell that she kept on a shelf close at hand and begin the tale.

We would be mesmerized of course, in rapt attention sitting on the bench by the old wooden baking table and with chocolate smeared on our faces. We especially loved the ones with lots of gore and dead bodies, like the story of the battle between the English and Spanish at the Castillo, or the one about witches being burned alive by religious zealots in old France. We would shriek with fright at the scary parts. Afterward, Grannie would clean our faces and we would run home to be scolded by our mother for being late.

"You haven't been bothering old Grannie, have you?" she would say, fixing us with a stare just like Grannie's. "Oh no," we would chorus, running up to our bedroom and trying not to laugh.

It wasn't until attending Flagler College that it had occurred to me how Grannie Shipley never seemed to be growing much older. There were classes to attend, girls to date, or gatherings with friends at the old pub on St. George Street to discuss politics and who was going to Daytona for Spring Break. There were fewer and fewer visits to the pastry shop.

One day I dropped by, sneaking in the back door out of habit, finding Grannie munching on a large slice of quiche pie. "Come in, I've been expected you," she said. "I have a special tale for you. I'm going on a trip and wanted to tell you this story before I leave for I may not return for some time." Then, after bringing me a large butter horn, she recited the traditional opening rhyme, rang the little bell and began.

It was a story about a young lady who could see into the future. She learned about herbs and healing and lived in England hundreds of years ago. In those days, she couldn't reveal her precognition powers as women who knew too much were considered witches who brought evil and pestilence. The townsfolk would often become superstitious and fearful, sometimes burning or drowning the clairvoyant. As she grew older, she wrote what she foresaw in a ballad, but kept it hidden for many years.

After the poem was published she faked her death, made her way to Spain and took passage to the New World, landing where some people, including an explorer called Ponce de Leon, claimed there was a fountain of youth. There were rumours about local natives who lived very long lives, perhaps even forever. Filled with curiosity, the woman investigated local native lore, searched out local springs and drank the waters but with no effect. While on her walks, however, she had gathered local herbs and edible plants, using them for medicine and trying them in different kitchen recipes. One plant in particular was very good in a quiche pie and it became a common part of her diet. To her surprise she didn't seem to age so long as she ate this particular type of pie.

"You see," Grannie said, finishing the story. "It wasn't the water but a local herb called Rosemorthorp that brought long life. And that particular herb only grows near water. Also, it is only effective when baked into a special quiche pie for which only that old woman had the recipe. She lived a long time and had many experiences. She may even be alive to this day."

Grannie left shortly thereafter and I never saw her again. I asked my mother what happened to her but I never received a straight answer. As it turned out, Mother Shipley wasn't even my real Grannie.

One Minute Mystery

Not Worth the Visit

By William Alan Gardner

I crept down the stairs to the poorly-lit basement, wishing Harry had installed the new light fixture as soon as we'd moved in. My night vision is good but not that good. The sounds were louder now and seemed to be coming from the far corner of the wall that divided our unit from the one next door. It was the darkest corner of the basement.

Perhaps I should have checked the place more carefully and thoroughly before the deal was signed but the realtor swore that the place was in terrific shape and the neighbours were quiet. Besides, at the time I thought investigating the upstairs and roof was more important. The first few weeks in the new place were great as we settled in, unpacking and getting all the furniture set up. I supervised beautifully.

Occasionally, and at odd hours, I would see the neighbours coming or going. And there were strange sounds—a kind of low pulsing vibration and a modulated

bzzzt, sort of like those high-voltage generator displays you see at science centers.
"It must be a TV program," Harry had said to me. "Maybe the neighbours are Trekkies and like to watch science fiction shows."

Today, while Harry was at work, I heard that repeating, rasping noise. It piqued my curiosity. I had to investigate.

The blackness of the basement closed around me, but as my eyes started to adapt I spied vague shapes clustered around what appeared to be a hole in the wall and one in the floor. A faint cerulean glow emanated from the floor and my nose started to itch, picking up a smell that reminded me of when the furnace motor in the previous house had overheated – that of ozone and electric insulation. The rasping noise stopped, replaced by a regular bzzzt, the same noise we'd heard before, but this time louder. The repetitions increased and were counterpointed by dim flashes of light. I crept closer, my feet making no sound on the concrete floor, and as I did, the shapes became more distinct, vaguely human, seemingly floating through the wall and descending into the hole in the floor. One of them turned and looked at me.

With that, my curiosity suddenly mutated into fear, bile pervading my mouth. I wanted to turn and run but my muscles wouldn't respond. With a rising sense of panic I stood there, frozen, hearing – if that's the proper word for it – the entities communicating. In a telepathic, conceptual way, I understood, and I even felt their emotions. They were aware of me and knew I was no threat. The last of them floated down into the hole, then a bump as if a hatch closed, then silence.

My paralysis disappeared and I raced upstairs, back to a familiar world that was suddenly less real than it had been a few moments ago. Under my feet began a low rumbling and the house began to shake. I flashed back to the neighbour's last intercepted thought. Even a cat could understand its meaning.

"Let's go Scottie, there's no intelligent life on this planet."

And Then There Were Tongues

By B. J. Thompson

"Bernie! Wake up! Bernieee...!"

Black X's for the eyes, tiny birdie tongue hanging out, Bernie wasn't going to wake up, ever. Bernie the baby birdie was DEAD. Dead, I say, and I should know. I'm Bert, Bernie's baby birdie brother.

We all woke up—Barney, Bailey, Becky and me—and saw Bernie just lying there... horrible site.

No one else was around, not even that awful Raven, Rob. He'd eat anything on the fly, he would.

Nope, it was just us birdies, and, of course Mom, all hanging out in our warm birdie nest, atop one of the two tallest trees in the neighbourhood.

It was awful. Bernie was gone. Oh, my... who would be next?

Next morning...
"Barney! No! Barney, wake up, will ya! That's not funny, stop playing games! Barneee!"

X's, dangling tongue, dislodged downy feathers wafting in the breeze. Barney was dead, too. It must have been overnight.

We Remaining Three looked at We Remaining Three with furtive, suspect glances. No black-tie dinner party in this nest, no nice, neat Agatha Christie ending here. We were dying, by numbers, and we were not amused.

Later in the birdie day...
Next door, the oak tree over from ours, baby Randy Robin had a teeny, weenie joystick in his weenie, teeny claw.

"Look, Bert! Look at what my Dad bought me! It's a teeny, tiny birdie PS4 and I'm playin' the latest game—Bird Kill 2.0! Man, you should see, is it ever realistic!"

~~~

The birdie neighbourhood went to Hell in a Hand-basket ever since our nests got electricity.
~~~

Last Call ~ Bar Scene

One More for the Road...

By B. J. Thompson

Joe's Tavern, Englewood Cliffs, New Jersey, 1937. Someone once said I channel Frank Sinatra, not my hero, Dean Martin, so like it or not, Sinatra is my soul-mate... I'll just have to get used to blended whiskey without ice and keep the fist-fighting down to a minimum...

~~~

Hey, Joe, set'em up for me, will ya? It's been a long, long road tonight."

"Sure thing, Frank, what's your poison?"

"Bad tips tonight, it better be the Jack. I can't afford the Johnny," Frank pulled up a stool, undid the top button of his shirt and yanked down his tie, fishing into his right jacket pocket for his pack of Lucky's.

Joe, the Bartender, grabbed the bottle off of the back shelf and was about to pour an ounce into a shot-glass when Frank interrupted his movement, saying, "No, Joe, hand me a tumbler. I'll keep the bottle. You keep that shot-glass clean."
~~~

Leaning forward with a fatherly look of concern, Joe asked, "What's eating at you tonight, kid? You've had bad nights before. Guests throw tomatoes at you when you were singing or something?"

"Nah, nuthin like that. Lemme tell ya a little story I think you oughta know..."

"Well, go on with ya then."

"I made a call, see, and well, you know that audition I did for Harry James down at Radio City? Well, he kicked me to the curb. I didn't get the gig," Frank said, as flick after flick he pulled down on his metal lighter—no flame. Joe reached into his apron pocket for his own lighter, igniting Frank's cigarette.

"Aw, well, listen kid, that ain't the end of the world. Try again in a couple years. You've just started singing with the Hoboken Four. Maybe you need more water flowing under that bridge of yours before you grab the Big Ring."

"Yeah...," Frank whispered, puffing on the cigarette loosely held between his thumb and index finger. The singer stared at the wooden floor, the aged boards stained with dirt, saliva, crusty blood and sticky booze. He feared this would be his end.

"You'd never know it, Joe, but I'm a kind of poet, and I've got a lot of songs I'd like to sing. But tonight, I'm gonna down this drink 'cause this burning need I've found, has gotta be drowned, or it soon might explode."

"I know, kid, I know. I've heard it all before from you crooners. How 'bout I turn on some real easy songs on the Wurlitzer and you make it one for your sorrow and one more for the road?"

"Thanks, Joe. Hey, I know, it's a quarter to three, 'n' no one in this place 'cept you and me, and you're gettin' ready to close. Thanks for the booze and thanks for listening, for me bending your ear."

"That's what I'm here for, kid. All you youngsters, you wanna make the Big Time, and then when things fall short, you wanna drown in bourbon. If it weren't for you kids, I'd not make a living."

Frank looked up with those piercing blue eyes and smiled, saying nothing.

A couple of minutes later, after taking several more puffs on his Lucky, the smoke rings billowing up, obscuring his face and the despondency within, Frank murmured, "I gotta make it as a saloon singer, Joe. I'm no good at anything else, and besides, my Ma, she's wantin' a crooner son if she can't have a priest."

Leaning over the bar and staring straight into the eyes of this diminutive Italian, Joe said, "Kid, you got The Voice, you keep diggin'. Go home. Alcohol is terrible for the vocal chords and you got another gig back here later tonight.
Gulping the last in his tumbler and pushing the empty glass towards Joe for him to fill one final time, Frank said, "Lets' make this one for Harry James and one more for the road."

Swigging it back in one go, Frank rose from the stool, affixed his Cavanaugh at a jaunty angle, swung his trench coat over his shoulder and headed for the door. The defeated saloon singer kept his head down and slumped his back, the smoldering cigarette dangling in his hand as he hit the wet pavement on a street abandoned to the wee hours. Mr. Nobody in the middle of Nowhere, New Jersey.

~~~

One More for the Road is a literary ode to Frank's saloon song, his best, in my opinion, One for My Baby (and One More for the Road)
~~~

Careful What You Order

By William Alan Gardner

The first shot was wide, ricocheting off the bar and smashing several bottles of cheap Aurelian ale. The bartender, a rather fine looking female robot didn't even flinch. I figured the bar might provide decent cover so I dived over it, bouncing unceremoniously off the floor and doing a quick shoulder roll to one side. I came up crouched using one hand on the glass washer to balance and yanking out my old but effective ARC21 with the other. I switched it to laser mode and put my back to the bar, watching the mirror on the back wall.

If anyone came leaning over the bar I'd see them before they could see me, so long as they weren't smart enough to check the reflection in the mirror too.

Sure enough the large Pleiadian soldier with a blaster who had been standing next to me, and had taken offence at my order, came peering over the bar to see if he could spot me. They never were known for their smarts. I aimed at his reflection in the mirror and the beam burned off half his face.

Earlier I'd seen him with a group of his bug-like buddies over in a corner booth horking down bowls of ... well, something we humans don't like to describe. Anyway, I knew his buddies wouldn't let this incident slide, even though he started the fracas. I reset the ARC21 to the Arclight setting and lobbed one toward the ceiling and over the bar, closing my eyes and raising my arm to shield. An Arclight is a special ball with a few atoms of antimatter surrounded by a magnetic field and a phosphorous shell. When it went off there wasn't much sound but the intensity of the light was enough to blind anyone without a blast helmet, at least for 20 earth minutes or so. It might even fry the ccd eye sensors in the bartender and that would really piss off the management, but I didn't see an easier choice. I always valued my neck more than a repair bill for some shmuck robot.

When the light subsided I rose and peered over the bar. Most of the patrons were incapacitated. Of course they'd reacted to the first shot by looking toward the bar – bad move on their part. I did a quick scan identifying the best escape route and any Grofian bouncers in my path. One of the Pleiadians was still active and had his blaster out.

He must have had his head down at the wrong – or right – moment, probably doing something disgusting to the female beside him, so had missed the worst of the flash. Fortunately for me he was looking toward the center of the bar where the bartender was standing and not at the far end of the bar where I was. That gave me a fraction of a second to switch my ARC21 – how I love that thing – to blaster mode and aim one in his direction. It caught him in the side and threw him back into the booth, crumpled and smoking. This place was going to smell real bad real soon.

I vaulted over the end of the bar and made a beeline for the exit. One shot barely missed me and splattered against the washroom door, burning a hole in the multicultural male icon. I made it into the alley, sprinting toward my [illegible] le. I flipped it into high accel, pushed the smoke [illegible] tton, and jacked the right handle to the limit. [illegible] onds later I was at the town limit having left a [illegible] cloud in my wake to ward off pursuers.

[illegible] thing had taken maybe four minutes from [illegible] dered the drink to when I passed the town limit sign. That bar will be off limits for a couple of weeks but, what the hell, there are others in this alien hellhole. And

I'll have to remember not to order an Anal Sex cocktail when I'm standing next to a Pleiadian grunt.

Last Call

By L. L. Sheppard

Lithe bodies undulated to the raucous beat, sweat streaked, all slamming into Vivian as she picked her way across the club's dance floor. The lights and smoke machine pulsed in time with the bass, making it impossible to clearly see the other side of the packed room.

I've gotta find him.

Vivian concentrated on moving through the drunken patrons to where he said his friends were sitting.

"Please, please be there," she pleaded to no one in particular. *God, he was hot.*

Drunken hands grabbed at her from the throng of frenzied dancers.

"Wanna dance?" a barely 18-year-old said, slurring his words and looking hopeful at his prospects as he swayed on his feet.

She smiled apologetically and motioned across the bar, "Just trying to find someone, sorry."

A shrug was all she received before he turned and asked the girl dancing beside her the same question.

Rude.

She shook her head and resumed her journey. After all, a better man waited.

Squeezing passed the last of the dancers, she burst into the lounge area almost knocking over a tray-laden waitress. Glasses clinked, and the trays teetered but the waitress was seasoned and caught her balance, not spilling a drop. She cast a dirty look at Vivian, and said, "Last call."

"Sorry, no thanks." Vivian said, raising her hands and backing up a step to let the woman pass.

Scanning the faces seated at the tables, her eyes settled on the guy who much earlier had asked her to dance. They danced so close, and after, his lips brushed her ear as he'd whispered, "Thank you." A shiver ran down her spine at the thought.

His attention was on his friend who was dancing around like a ballerina; the entire group laughing and making fun of their jester.

I can't do this, he's way too hot!

As if he read her thoughts, his eyes snapped to hers. The smile that spread to every muscle in his face lit up the room like the fourth of July.

"Finally," he mouthed the word from across the table.

Her heart skipped a beat. *He's happy I'm here!*

He stood, excusing himself from his friends and strode easily the fifteen feet, taking up her hand, "Wanna get out of here?"

"Sure." She beamed up at him, and he led her towards the exit.

Blinding lights assaulted her eyes, and she squinted over at her handsome suitor. He smiled back at her.

What the... Did he always have eyelashes just on one eye? Is that a patch of missing hair on the side of his head?

Is... is that guacamole in his teeth?

What have I done, oh God!

"Um... I forgot...," she tried to think of an excuse, "I have to dog sit and, well, the dog is, um... waiting! Yeah. So... I should go! Sorry!"

Vivian untangled her fingers from his and hurried out into the night.

Last Call

By Rob Richards

A flickering neon sign over the dented and rusted metal door situated at the end of the alley identifies the establishment as, "The Keyhole."

With Electric Avenue succumbing to the same gentrification as the rest of downtown Calgary, sketchy watering holes such as this were becoming more and more elusive. You grin at me, pushing open the door and we enter the dark, stinking hellhole.

Bathed in an angry red light and half cast in shadow, the bar vibrates with the murmur of whispered conversation. Wooden masks carved to resemble misshapen demonic faces hang on the walls. Eyes flick in our direction as we approach the bar. Heather, the bartender, greets us with a single arched eyebrow, the crimson light glinting off her multiple facial piercings. Her tattoos seem to swim across her skin in the gloom. The evening's entertainment is already underway–some no-name band from a small town in the middle of butt fuck nowhere. All wailing vocals, screeching guitar and migraine-inducing drum solos. No talent, but enough edge to scalp a Rastafarian.

"You're late," Heather says, plopping down a pair of tequila shots in front of us.

"Bitch, please. There's still plenty of time," you reply, passing me one of the shots.

"Bottoms up, babe."

We pound back the shots and you direct your attention to the band onstage. I pull out my grandfather's black-handled knife and start carving intricate curlicues into the bar top. Heather glares at me.

"Fucking really, dude?"

I ignore her. The act of petty vandalism helps to drown out the crowd, the music, and the knowledge of what happens next. The band has finished their set. I glance up and see that you've already gone to speak with them. Heather has gone as well, presumably to lock the doors. I fix my attention back on my carving. This would be so much easier if I didn't have to look at them.

As the shouting and sounds of a scuffle erupt behind me, I try to distract myself by admiring my grandfather's knife; the well-worn handle wrapped in disquieting black leather, the finely honed steel blade, the pommel shaped like a snarling goat's head...

Your voice drags me, kicking and screaming, back into reality. The rite has begun.
Several burly men have forced the band members onto their knees, pinning their hands behind their backs and holding their heads over polished brass bowls. I stand and take my place next to you as you recite a litany of verses in a language no one in their right mind would ever learn. Something about ancient gods and sacrifice you told me long ago when we held one another under a canopy of stars. With a sweep of your hand, you finish your incantation and step back. Now it's my time to shine.

I crouch next to the first lamb to be slaughtered. My stomach is doing somersaults and my heart pounds to break free. Even after three years, I'm still not used to this. I look into the young man's eyes, trying to convey an apology. I dare not speak, lest I suffer a fate far worse than his.

As I swing my blade, slashing open the bassist's jugular, I wish that we had gotten here earlier. A couple more drinks would have helped to take the edge off.

Siblings

I Slay a Slew of Siblings

By B.J. Thompson

It wasn't my fault. They got in my way. I could have endured being the black sheep of the Family... if I were an only child...

Susan, oh Susan, you were the light of our family's life, until I ran you over with Clarence, our lead Clydesdale. Now you're black and blue, and dead all over. Your bruises emit a nice glow, all the same.

Irene, I didn't want to say goodnight, but when your pitch fork got stuck in the generator... while you were holding it... well, now you're the new light of our family... however dead the coroner says you are.

Betty, we called you Elizabeth for short, until the rope from our swing set got accidentally wrapped around your neck... four times... now we call you Long Liz. It has a ring to it, don't ya think?

Lucille, it wasn't a fine time to leave me, but it's not like I planned to run you over when I put the tractor into Drive. I probably meant to when I slid it into Reverse though... sorry about that.

Ian, poor wee Ian. I knew you needed that wooden leg to walk. Why, oh why, did I think it would make a great fishing pole... with you still attached? I thought it was a trout pond, not a tarantula pit! My eyes aren't what they used to be...

Nancy, oh Nancy, our family poet divine. Now, you know you were never a favourite mine, so when that sinkhole appeared, you fit just so fine.

Gordon, hey Gord, don't blame me. It was my ball, and I was going home. I'd had enough of your winning streak. It's not like you'd be playing any longer anyhow with that baseball bat wedged into your skull.

Sarah, oh sweet Sarah, the last of the bunch. Our poet replacement for Nancy, but now you, too, are dead. Lunch... time!

A Photographer & a Sniper Meet in a Bar

The Patient Man

By Iva Polansky

The bar was just the place where Ron needed to be, dehydrated as he was after the last couple of days. He ordered a beer, gulped it in one go, and asked for a margarita. This drink he sipped slowly while looking around. Not many chicks; all of three sat at a large table where nearly every male wore an outfit composed of some military cast-off. The weekend warriors were shooting selfies. Not exactly a crowd that would appreciate the effort that went into getting pictures worthy of the National Inquirer.

Ron obviously stared too long, for a man from the group got up and, carrying his beer, approached the bar.

"You new here? You here for shooting?" he asked while plopping his rear end on the stool next to Ron.

"Shooting?" Ron shook his head. "Nah, I've done enough shooting for the day. You'll read about it soon. I got that cheating bitch at last," he named a married movie actress, "caught them both, she and her paramour. Took me nearly two days. That's the key to this business, you know. Patience."

The man's posture changed, becoming rigid. "Really?"

Ron nodded, glad to have an audience for his triumph. "Once you find where your targets are, you just stay put, out of sight, for as long as it takes. Day and night, you wait for the right opportunity. You get used to long stints after a while. When I'm after someone, I make sure to pack some food and a thermos of coffee. And a bottle to pee in if I sit in the car. That's crucial. You don't want to miss the right moment."

The man swallowed, his Adam's apple popping up and down. "Nice talking to you," he said, sliding off the bar stool.

Ron went to pee, ordered another margarita upon his return, and cast a look into the mirror behind the barman, who was drying glasses with a dingy tea towel. In a bar filled with people and blaring music, he suddenly felt alone. In the reflection, Ron saw his interlocutor was back at the table where nobody moved and everybody was staring straight at him. Unbeknownst to Ron, one of the party pocketed a mobile after dialling a three-digit number.

"What a strange dude," Ron said to the barman. "So friendly at first and then he cuts me short. Some manners! You know him?"

The barman picked up another glass and began to rub it with the towel. "He's okay," he said. "He's the owner of the shooting range down in the basement."

The Lens Factor...

By B.J. Thompson

In the dark, dank and stale beer-infused Dusty's, a seedy watering hole on the north side of Washington, DC, sat two men at the bar. Each arrived looking lonely or maybe introspective, both rather annoyed that their wrists were sticking to the bar surface. Glancing across, seeing their mutual disgust, the men joined forces on two side-by-side stools.

"Christ, you think this joint ever sees a goddamned wash cloth?" asked Steve, as he rifled through his large carry-on case for a lens wipe.

"Fuckin' doubtful, man. Hey, I'm Mengen, what's yours?" as he reached over to shake the hand of this rather well-dressed cleanliness freak.

"Steve. Steve Largent."

Silence reigned as the men hunkered down to sip their scotch-rocks.

Breaking the spell, Steve said, "Man, I don't usually hit joints like this but my tail is in a crack right now, and I don't want the up-towners to see me squirm."

"Oh, yeah. What about?" asked Mengen, not really interested, as he had his own shit to shuffle.

"I have to get a shot tomorrow, and a good one, or I'll be demoted to targets that don't pay and will sink my rep."

Mengen's ears twigged, and offered, "Well, I'll be damned. A fellow shooter. I got to nail a sucker dead-to-rights tomorrow, too, or the contract goes to this schmuck I know in Jersey and that asshole couldn't hit the broadside of Oprah."

The men laughed. Mengen caught the eye of the bartender and ordered two more.

"Oh, so you're a shooter, too. Well, that's a coincidence right there. Who you work for?" asked Steve, already sweating under his collar that the competition found him. "Uh... I'm free-lance. What about you?"

"I'm in-house at–"

Some bikers walked by, bumping into Steve, the fear stopped cold his sentence.

Looking up, and sensing Steve's fear, Mengen swapped questions, "Your gig is tomorrow, huh? What's your plan?"

"Uh, the usual. Get there before dawn, settle into an unseen shooter's nest, set the zoom, and wait."

Mengen appreciated the method. It was his. The two men gulped the last of their drinks and departed.

Five a.m. the next morning...

Throngs of well-wishers lined the route. In an abandoned lot many yards away, cordoned off with chain-link and sequestered by feral bushes, Steve would lie in wait. His zoom lens would fit perfectly through the links, and he was sure he'd get off a perfect shot of the President elect as he made his way out the side portico exit on his way to the inauguration stand at Capitol Hill.

Steve heard a rustling. To his shock, he spied Mengen, already nestled in *his* lair. Both men had the same lens. Steve's would capture the million dollar shot for TIME magazine.

Mengen's, however, was sitting atop an XM500 Barrett.50 Cal "Light Fifty" sniper rifle that could shoot to kill through a wall at 2600 meters. He would get his cool million another way.

All that was said, was said by Steve.

"Move over."

Shots

By William Alan Gardner

When Phoebe slid onto her usual bar stool, settling her hips onto the cushion, there were few eyes that didn't cast a glance her way. The bartender sensed the slight reduction in conversation as she arrived and was ready with her standard: a shot of Jäger followed by a double martini with two olives and a twist of lime, not lemon. Usually she wore a paisley dress but tonight her slim frame was wrapped in a form-fitting khaki shirt, a brown hunter's vest and dusty jodhpurs that belled out at the hips. The effect emphasized her figure. Tall leather boots completed the outfit and made her look like she had just ridden in from a week on the veldt.

She threw back the shot and took a sip from the martini before bothering to look around. It was classic Phoebe. Half the men in the bar were in love with her and the other half would have crawled a mile over acacia thorns to spend a night in her company. Normally the clientele were local town folk and a few familiar bushmen. Tonight she noticed a stranger a couple of stools away at the bar.

He was casually dressed in tan slacks and a light blue golf shirt, looking like a tourist dwankie who'd wandered into the wrong bar. Curious, Phoebe stared at him. For a moment the man stared back. Picking up his bottle of Castle Lager, he sauntered over and sat beside her.

"Shoot much?" he said, taking a swig from the bottle.

"Some," she replied, waving her hand around to indicate the bar walls which were festooned with stuffed heads of lion, kudu, impala and other animals plus a set of excellent framed photographs of landscapes and wildlife. "And you?"

"Jah, usually further north. Kenya was good but I thought I'd try for a few around here. There's a good market for my stuff in the States." Despite his evident American accent he had already adopted some of the slang."By the way, my name's Dieterich, or just Dieter to my friends." He held out his hand and she took it briefly, noticing the firm grasp.

"Phoebe," she said. "Been here in Nels long? I haven't seen you before." She surveyed him, noticing that despite the dwankie outfit he was certainly fit.

Something about this guy doesn't jibe, too confident, too aware.

"Just flew in yesterday from Joburg. I've arranged a guide to show me some great shooting locations. He said he had a blind by a waterhole. I can nail them from a distance but I prefer to be as close as possible to avoid problems when the light is wrong." He noticed that she had finished her martini. "Can I buy you another?"

Pausing as if to consider the wisdom of accepting, she replied slowly. "Okay."

Dieter signalled the bartender who gave him a scowl before attending to the order.

"So you've done quite a bit of shooting yourself evidently," he said, turning to look at the bar walls. "You must have lived here a long time. Do you know the owner? His brown eyes turned back to Phoebe, trying not to look at the curve of her breasts straining under the shirt. "I'd be interested in seeing your equipment." *Shit, a Freudian slip.* He blushed at the thought, realizing what he'd just said. "Ahh, I mean your shooting equipment of course. What did you use to get that one?" He pointed toward a beautifully composed photograph of a group of impala and an elephant at a watering hole with the silhouette of an acacia tree and streaks of red sunset. It hung next to a Cape Buffalo head. He wasn't prepared for her answer. "A Springfield 03," she said. It's old but extremely accurate and reliable. The 30-06 cartridge puts them down fast. You never have to worry about tracking a wounded animal. That Buff up there." she indicated the head of the particularly mean-looking Cape Buffalo beside the photograph, "He went down like he'd been hit with a tank round. Not like the Hemingway story. It was a great hunt. What do you use?"

"You shoot them?" Dieter's face clicked through a variety of expressions. Finally he said, "Well, my favorite is the Nikon 7000 with an Opteka 650-1300 telephoto zoom."

Then he laughed.
A moment later, Phoebe started to laugh, too.
Dieter paused long enough to order another round.

The Key

The Magic Key

By William Alan Gardner

The flying bug bounced once as it landed in the grassed field near Mathina's small hut. Waiting in the sun-dappled shadows of the adjacent forest she heard it arrive and roll to a stop. She fought the conflict in her mind - the desire to share in the power and knowledge he possessed, and the feeling of powerlessness and envy he brought in controlling the air whirler - and her. She longed for his company, yes, but her soul yearned even more to take the air machine, to be set free and escape her lonely fate. It was a forbidden thought but she toyed with it nonetheless. As a witch she understood power, for it was her powers that drove her from the village and into isolation.

Loneliness and power circle one another like the two ravens that she kept as familiars. But power without action was useless, and the exercise of real power requires planning.

She stepped out from the trees and walked slowly toward him as he turned the air whirler around and crawled out of the seat and onto the grass. She lowered her eyes in respect and to help hide her feelings.

"Greetings my lord," she said simply but with a firm voice.

"You are well, Matti?" he asked.

Mathina watched as he leaned back into the machine and withdrew the small talisman from where it fitted into the front wall near the seat. When she had asked about it previously he had called it a key. Whatever its name, she understood that it was a magic object to enable the air whirler to ride up into the wind.

"Well enough my Lord. How was your journey?" she said, raising her eyes to his, looking to read any message in his expression.

"Clear air and striding." He smiled. "I have something for you." He hung the talisman around his neck and then turning, retrieved a small package from behind the seat. It was wrapped in cloth dyed with the sacred color blue, almost a sacrilege. Regardless, she stepped forward and received it, again lowering her head as she did so.

"What is it?" She asked.
"Some special soap I thought you would like. They make it in a village a few valleys over. It has a nice fragrance."

He paused and then walked to her.

"Do you have any of your special tea? It has been a long flight."

He encircled her waist with his arm, bent down and kissed her, tasting the slight aroma of caraway. Mathina returned the kiss, both wanting and resenting it, then broke free and led him to her hut. She pushed her conflict down deep into her belly.

The interior of the hut was simple, two rooms and a loft where she slept. One room served for herbal mixing and storage, and was her healing place for villagers when they visited with common ailments. The other served as a kitchen with a counter, cupboards and a simple table for meals. Everything was neat and tidy. The air inside carried a rich variety of smells that brought images of the deep forest, of peat and rot and regrowth, both clean and complex. The man sat down in the larger chair, one she had made especially for him, and straightened his back, stretching and inhaling deep.

"I almost didn't come today. Icarus is acting up and I'm almost out of fuel. There's just enough to get back to San Pedro. But I missed you. Why must you live in this godforsaken forest?"

He chatted on about things outside her world, about things she didn't understand, using words that held no meaning. She tended the fire, bringing water to a boil and adding the herbs for tea, plus a special ingredient. They drank it together, saying little. Then she led him to her bed, she being comfortable in her own silence, and he with his own need.

Afterward, when he was in a deep sleep she took the talisman from around his neck, slipped into her forest clothes, and walked out to the air machine. Seating herself she slipped the metal key into the slot and pushed the button as she had seen her lord do. Grasping the stick she pushed forward. Her ignorance was not lack of ability and soon she had it in the air.

Up and up she went, out of the darkness of the trees and valley, up toward the sun, leaving all that she knew behind. She exalted in the freedom, the sense of being a god herself and looking down at the world from the clouds. Upward she flew as a raven circles upward on thermal *shafts, and then out past the hills, beyond even her imagination. I can reach the sun, she thought as the world below her shrank.*

I am free.

She lost track of time in her newfound freedom until there was a sudden silence, and then falling, spiralling down to the earth and trees rushing toward her.

The Key

By B.J. Thompson

A late arrival for me into the quaint Town of Beausejour, Manitoba.

The drive from Kakabeka Falls to south central Manitoba took longer than I had anticipated. So with droopy eyelids and a weary body, I checked into the Best Western for a well-deserved night's rest.

With a dead sleep, an instant awakening is often the result. I blinked my eyes—3:00—in the red glowing alarm clock a.m. I rose from my covers and padded over to the window, its view facing west and into the wee hamlet which stood silent still, its prairie inhabitants well asleep.

A walk and some fresh air will do the trick, I mused, for although my mind was content to be back in my mother's home town, disquieting thoughts were a swirl in my head, of times past, good, and bad. Upon meeting up with the road-sign, "Beausejour Population 3,126", a wall of fog, or what I thought was fog, hit me. It twinkled and danced, and upon my exit of it, I turned around and it was gone... like it had never been.

The sidewalks straddling the main drag of Park Avenue were vacant, the light standards aglow but with no humanity under them upon whom to shine. As I strode past the "Nip & Chip" shop, a sound, a kind of "clang-bang-clang" hit my ears. I stopped, listened. Moments later, another. Several rounds of this alien noise with only a minute or two separating each. A moment more, and a black silhouette, manly in stature, appeared on the sidewalk, its long legs coming closer, its footfalls, a strident step, threatening to become a march.

"Dad, it's you?"

"Yes, Barbie, it's me."

"What are you doing here? You're..."

"I'm on foot patrol, checking store front locks, making sure the town is secure for the night."

Our paths drew close, my eyes locking onto his form. That of a much younger man than I remembered, dressed in the work blue serge uniform with all its Constable insignia, the unmistakable beige Stetson at a jaunty angle a top his Brylcreem-laden hair.

"I hear you've done security work."

"Yes, Daddy, I wanted to know what it was like to be you."

"I hear you've taken down and arrested criminals."

"Yes, Daddy."

"Did you shoot your weapon?"

"No weapon, Dad, unless you count a holstered Bear Spray."

A moment's pause...

"I see..."

A moment more...

"I miss you, Daddy."

"Ich liebe dich," said my father, for emotions had to remain in a foreign tongue, distant, so as not to hurt. "Go back now, Barbie. It's time for you to return."

"But you, and now Mom? I..."

"Lock us away in your mind, Barbie. The key to Life is living it while you can," he said, as he lifted a special gold key for me to see from the many on his chain.

As soon as the key appeared, it faded from view, along with the dearly missed image of my father.

The Key

By Christianne Parrott

A true story narrative.

May 16, 1966

He first heard about the declaration from a hushed voice in the dark and knew that he must act immediately or risk being killed.

For some time, he had felt uneasy with this new political movement, their ideologies seemed horribly misguided, doomed to bring grief to the people it claimed to protect. He could see through the charade of speeches and rallies that those uninitiated could not—all lies, deception, manipulation and a lust for power. Alas, the masses were smitten with their beloved saviour. They believed, and wanted to believe, he could save them all and bring might and glory to their beautiful nation. They never considered the cost.

All day long, he sensed something was wrong, that something horrible was about to happen. He felt it behind his navel—the seat of his intuition—so he was prepared when he heard the news. He already packed a few small items, none overly valuable, but to him, priceless. After dinner, he changed into plain clothes, the urgency in his belly quickening as the day wore on.

The time had come. He would flee, for if he died, the life's work and the secret knowledge of hundreds of doctors who had come before would be lost; the medicine of the people would be gone. His was a secret lineage, bound to follow, protect and preserve the true understanding of medicine as it was handed down by Zhang Zhong Jing himself. This lineage held the secret key necessary to understand the ancient texts. Without this key there was confusion, missing pieces, and unanswerable questions; with the key, all could be treated and none abandoned.

He left the palace with no more than the clothes on his back, those few belongings, and a fierce determination to stay alive and preserve the lineage. He was the last imperial doctor and he would not fail.

He moved his once prominent life into the background, keeping himself and his knowledge secret from those who would destroy it. The revolutionary years were painful and filled with fear and secrecy. He watched as countless friends and colleagues disappeared, were murdered or sent to work camps, often turned in by those closest to them. He would not be caught, nor would he let his lineage end.

He mostly kept to himself, sharing his work with the youngest of children, teaching them rhymes and sayings to help them learn new words and arcane knowledge. They were too young to realize the information was old, older than the trees in the forest and the ancient buildings of the city.

And so, the key was kept secret, locked in the minds of the young, until one day they would find the door that it would open.

Elevator Ride with Someone

The Elevator Ride

By L. L. Sheppard

"There are two of us here!" I shouted into the elevator emergency phone. I looked over my shoulder at the woman, but unlike me, she looked calm, unperturbed even...

"Hello!? Can anyone hear me?" I bellowed.

The woman stared at me with a smug-looking smile plastered on her face.

Oh God, she's going to kill me. Her cold eyes looked into mine.

This is how it all ends. They've finally found out my secrets, and she's been sent to dispatch me, just like I figured. How am I going to get out of this? How can I get away? Oh, my God, they've stopped the elevator on purpose! Why is there nothing I can use as a weapon in here?

My heart beat skipped amid the racing. I wiped my sweaty palms across my thighs but it did little to alleviate the clamminess. Beads of cold sweat broke out on my brow and rolled in thin rivulets down my blanched face.

This is it. For sure, this is the end. I should never have looked, never have overheard, but I did, and now I will end up dead. Dead! Oh God... this is really happening, isn't it?

Sheer panic overtook me. That hot, sick feeling slipped down my spine and invaded my entire body. My vision blurred and funneled to a pin point. My hearing dampened and my ragged breath sounded like it belonged to someone else, someone who lived inside an empty fish bowl. I pounded the button.

"Can anyone hear me!" I pleaded into the tiny box.

I darted a glance back at the woman to make sure she hadn't moved, but she was still standing there... assessing. Quiet. Controlled.

Why isn't she doing anything? What is she going to do? What is she waiting for? Oh, my God Just get it over with already! Oh please, oh please, don't kill me! How can I get out of here? How can I get away from her? What's she going to do?

The woman closed in behind me. My stomach spiralled downward and dizziness overtook so that I thought I would pass out.
There's not enough air. The walls were closing in.

Staggering forward, I reached again for the button...

Ding!

The elevator doors slid open, and a disembodied voice announced "Psychiatric Ward, 9th Floor."

"That's enough nonsense Bill, back to your room. This way please," the woman said, as she took my arm and led me away.

Elevator Going Up?

By B. J. Thompson

Quitting time in the Capital Block Building was seven hours ago.

Audrey pushed the button to go down to the Lobby. A glutton for punishment, she was, working all hours despite her utter exhaustion, but with an easy commute now that half the city was already home and in bed.

The red light dimmed, the ding sounded, and the doors parted.

Audrey was not alone.

Another workaholic was also calling it quits at the witching hour.

Stepping in, Audrey felt sure she recognized the woman, but with no Hello and her face downcast, she couldn't be sure.

Audrey sensed a prickling of her skin, and that she was being watched by this other employee. She forced herself not to look back, for being too pushy, too curious, or God forbid, too rude in the corporate world were standard No-Nos at any hour.

The vibration began, and the elevator hummed along on its journey. A few minutes later, the cab stopped cold, the elevator lights died, and the doors remained shut. Audrey turned around to see the other passenger but in the darkness she could not make out her face. She thought she saw a faint glimmer of a smile but no words came, her elevator buddy quite disturbingly silent.

With a sigh, Audrey turned back and with fumbling fingers found the Red Button, slammed it hard with her palm, picked up the emergency phone, and shouted, "Hello, is anyone there? We're stuck in, uh, Otis Elevator #3 in the Capital Block Building downtown. Can you help us? There's two of us here."

Audrey looked over her shoulder at the woman. Unlike her own demeanour, the unknown woman looked calm, remained still.

There was a hum, then a popping sound, then a tone so beautiful, so clear and pure. A serene voice broke the air, "Yes, of course, I can help. The stall isn't mechanical. All you need to do is to Accept, stop fighting, and the doors will open."

"What do you mean, Accept, stop fighting? I haven't done a thing. The cab just stopped on its own. We haven't done anything."

"See, my dear, you said We. There is no We. There is only you. Turn around, let her go, and the doors will open."

Audrey, by now rather perturbed but desperate to get free of this metal box by any means, did as she was told and turned around to interact with the stranger. But upon viewing her face for the first time, the air from Audrey's lungs vacated and the fear of fainting threatened to down her.

The woman was no stranger at all. As she raised her head, Audrey knew that face all too well. It was her own. She was looking at herself. The image threw Audrey against the doors, the urge to scream suppressed only by her raging fear.

"Oh, my God, what's going on here? Get me out of here!"
"Say, I Accept, and the doors will open."

"I Accept! I Accept!"

And the doors did open. And her corpse crumpled to the lobby floor.

Audrey died of a heart attack in that elevator. A massive coronary which killed her body, had her spirit still fighting for more.

As her soul walked out into the light, Muzak within the fading elevator could be heard playing.

It was Bob Dylan's Knockin' on Heaven's Door.

Elevator Ride

By Christianne Parrott

Constance entered the glossy lobby at a brisk pace, her stilettos giving off an air of importance to those inside. She made a straight line to the elevator; head high, long strides, and though none were in her way, a path cleared before her. Elevator doors slid open at her approach. She boarded and pressed her floor button all in one economical movement.

A briefcase thrust itself into the narrowing gap, disrupting the perfection of her entrance.

Constance laid eyes on the briefcase wielder. His smile was soft and easy as he met her steady gaze. Turning the wrong way, he missed the button panel. Four steps more, and his gloved hand hovered up and down the neat rows before pressing the eighth-floor button. He stepped back and faced forward, switching the briefcase from one hand to the other. The doors closed for a second time.

Constance was certain she had seen his face before in a similar setting. The strangeness of the connection stimulated her mind, and it began flipping through all elevator associated memories, searching for one that contained his face. *Click, click, click.* This particular elevator featured familiar faces and only a few strange ones. His was not among them.

By the fifth floor, her mind had reviewed every face on every elevator of every building she frequented in the country. He was a match for none, yet his familiarity lingered. That face was connected somehow to elevators. She just had to find the right one.

His free hand slipped into his pocket as they neared the seventh floor. She remained still, ever prepared. As the elevator slowed, he moved to the door, keys in hand. Her breathing slowed as she waited.

Ping. Swoosh. He stepped out.

On the ninth floor, a second person entered with an arm full of boxes. "Can you press the 15th please?"

This face sparked no triggers in her mind, so she pressed the desired floor and they continued up in silence. Her

mind still flipping through faces and places and any other possible elevator connections she found.
Video footage. Click. There he was, standing beside Stan, a now deceased colleague.

Nothing unusual, no contact or conversation between the two had occurred. He had entered the elevator after Stan, scanned the buttons in the same manner, and departed on a lower floor.

Click. Click. Boom!

Stan had also pressed a floor button for an unknown box-wielding elevator goer, then died of a heart attack. Cause unknown. Her heart beat increased and sweat formed on her brow.

She exited on the 12th, clutched her shoulder and fell, dead.

Elevator Abduction

By William Alan Gardner

"There's two of us here!"

I shouted into the elevator emergency phone.

I looked over my shoulder at the woman. Unlike me, she looked calm, unperturbed even. I turned to the phone again with a rising feeling of anger.

"Hello, hello!" I waited.

Finally a soothing feminine voice on the other end of the line said "Thank you for your call. You have reached the office of the Ministry of Elevator Services. The office is currently closed. Please call back during our office hours of..."

I aborted the message and slammed the handset into its cradle.

"What the fuck," I yelled. "I knew this would happen after they nationalized all the building maintenance companies. Those assholes are trying to get us to walk up the stairs instead of taking the elevator."

"It's to save energy and make us better," said the woman behind me. "Everything they do is to make us better and more efficient. There's no need to get upset or angry. Here, just take one of these." She fumbled in her purse and handed me a green pill. "You'll feel so much better." She had a Mona Lisa smile and her eyes, green like the pill, were looking at me with perfect, calm condescension. She pulled a mickey flask out of her purse.

"By the way, I'm Rachel," she said with a slight up-tick in her voice. The flask was made of some sort of green glass. As I took it our hands touched and I noticed her delicate, almost picture-perfect fingers. She smiled, and I couldn't help noticing her cleavage as she leaned forward. "It's all right," she said reassuringly. "It will just relax you. What's your name?"

"I'm Richard. Do you work in the building?" I noticed her perfume. It had a slight scent of flowers and coconut and it reminded me of my last beach holiday. My eyes scanned her face trying to decide if she was a Pregen or a Newgen. It was hard to tell these days. As a man you had to be careful.

"Oh yes, I work on floor twenty two in the Ministry of Placidity. I usually leave work right on time but we were dealing with the protein riots and I had to stay late writing reports. Those poor people in Freedom Square were getting so angry! They were about to harm themselves but we intervened, just in time. Placigas is so effective and calming. They'll be just fine now."

I stared at her. "Well, what the hell," I thought, popping the pill into my mouth and taking a swig from the flask. Besides, getting stuck in an elevator with a foxy lady wasn't the worst thing that had happened to me this week. The liquid had a slight licorice taste, a bit like Jagermeister. A warmth spread downward from my throat to my belly and a sudden feeling of calm happiness spread along the nerve pathways upward to my brain. My muscles relaxed and I had to grab the rail to keep steady.

"Wow, that feels great," I murmured, leaning toward her. Through a slight haze I noticed that she now had a key and was doing something with the elevator controls. The elevator lurched upward and then the doors opened into a small room with computers and blinking monitors. Rachel had my hand and was leading me past the monitors. One of them had a Ministry logo. I was feeling relaxed and happy. Nothing is wrong. This is absolutely the right thing. Yes, how could anything that feels so good be bad? My mind noticed the words on the screen as I passed it. They spelled out 'Ministry of Human Improvement' around the logo. It glowed green. There was something familiar about that colour.

The warmth was increasing, moving downward again until I felt it pulsing and hot between my legs. Was the pill causing that, or the drink? Rachel was so good looking, especially with no clothes. No clothes!? I heard her speaking to the other person. It seemed a long way off as Rachel helped me onto the bed.

"His DNA is just what we needed," she was saying. "We will add it to our own. We were lucky to find a suitable male. There are so few of them nowadays. Have you prepared the other females?"

Adultery

The Family Business

By Iva Polansky

The man could have been handsome some thirty years ago. Even now he had a certain charm with his salt and pepper hair and a good suntan. The salt and pepper was mostly salt now, but Tanya could imagine him a strong forty with the gray just creeping in at the temples. She had a weakness for this kind of look in a man. Derek was the same type, but with all the glory of his early twenties added to the picture. Except that Derek would cost her dearly now.

"Who will guarantee me that it's one time only?" she asked. "Once I pay you, you could come back asking for more."

They were sitting in a Starbuck's café with the rain beating down on the plate-glass window. The man stirred sugar into his cappuccino. "I'm afraid that our firm cannot offer a written guarantee. You'll have to rely on our word."

"Your firm? Are you kidding me, you sleaze bag?"

"Careful, madam. Insults may cost you. In any case, you don't have much choice. It's common knowledge that your husband's tired of you. Your looks are not of the freshest these days, you have to admit. Since you had to sign a prenup, you won't get a red cent if the divorce is your fault."

He extended his hand for the envelope pinned to the table by Tanya's arm. She opened her mouth to protest anew, then sighed and released the pressure. The envelope disappeared smoothly into the man's breast pocket.

"There," the man said, "fear not. There are enough aging gold diggers in this country to make a good living asking just once. We're not heartless, you know."

With this, the man left, and Tanya hoped never to see him again. She was furious. Not only did the blackmailer ask for a pile of money, but she did not have Derek anymore to soothe her sorrows. He left without telling her and then sent her an old-fashioned post card from Arizona, saying that he had gotten a job offer he could not refuse. As if the wages of a tennis coach was worth leaving Toronto! She had planned a trip to Arizona with the intent of finding him and having it out, but that was no longer safe. There was this man, this blackmailer, knowing far too much and being able to cash in on it. No, this was the end of Derek.

The end of a passion. The end of all happiness. She felt tears coming.

Tanya met Derek once more. She was visiting her sister in Winnipeg and had promised her nephews a trip to Dairy Queen. As they were digging into their banana splits, she heard that sexy voice again, saying, "Chocolate or strawberry, Dad?"

She turned abruptly. It was Derek, there was no mistake. The man he was talking to was the blackmailer.

Adultery

By Christianne Parrott

A muffled thump and rustle woke me out of a not so deep sleep. I jumped out of bed, beyond excited. I couldn't believe my luck!

I had slept fully clothed, completely prepared for such a situation. Silencing slippers shod, I raced downstairs, making sure that I went unnoticed by the Big Man below.

On the staircase landing, I froze. The scene in the living room was beyond my six-year-old comprehension. There was Santa, in all of his red and white glory, on TOP of my mom.

What was he doing on top of mom?
Where was dad?
What... why... were they kissing!
No, no, no No!

I crept silently backwards up to my room and into bed. My head was spinning as my stomach tied itself into ten thousand knots. What kind of nightmare had I woken up to? All I really wanted to know was how Santa got into and out of the house!

My mind started racing with questions, grasping for any possible explanation of the depraved scene I had just witnessed.

Did Santa not like the cookies and somehow needed another form of payment?
Or, did he like the cookies so much he was trying to get mom to go back to the North Pole with him?
Was mom Mrs. Claus in secret? Like Batman but for Christmas? Had my wish list been too long?
What would dad think? Or did he even know? What if he did know and was okay with it? What would that mean? Was dad somewhere with Mrs. Claus? Oh God no! Did he kiss everybody's mom? What about the kids that only had dads?
Did this mean that we were moving to the North Pole and I'd have to live with the elves and reindeer? If snowmen could talk in the North Pole, it might be worth it. I had never met talking snow before.

And on and on it went until morning when I finally heard a knock on the door. I was ready for anything. Fearing the worst but hoping for the best, I got out of bed and opened the door. My dad looked down at me with a twinkle in his eye, and with great enthusiasm advised me that there were presents for me under the tree… from Santa.

My heart sunk. He didn't know, and I didn't know how to tell him.

Mattress Master

By B.J. Thompson

An immaculate, well-appointed master bedroom at 555, 5th Avenue & 57 Street, Manhattan, circa late '60s.

The hue: eggshell-white everything—walls, furniture, bedspread, broadloom, drapes.
The decor: contemporary.
The lightning: bright, but soft—a stand lamp and two side table lamps furnished a pleasant illumination on a rather unpleasant conversation.

Gladys sat at her dressing table in a slinky silk negligee, slowly brushing out her hair-sprayed Do as Irvin lay in bed, horn-rimmed eye glasses adorned, reading the Wall Street Journal. A Pall-Mal cigarette, the final one of his busy day, smoldering in a heavy bottle-glass ash tray encased in a solid silver stand to his right...

"Irvin."

"Yes, dear."

"I know what's been going on. I'm not blind. I know what you've been doing. All those late night work hours, stumbling in at dawn, all those long, liquid lunches when your secretary says you're unavailable to take my call. I find the swizzle sticks and the match boxes and those out-of-place feathers stuck inside your jacket pockets. Feathers, Irvin? Really? How gauche. No real woman would tolerate feathers..."

Gladys's voice trailed off into nothing, as if all her mental power had ebbed away with each stroke of her hair that heavy silver hairbrush made.

Irvin said not. He noisily refolded the Journal to the next page, but this time, rose the paper ever so slowly into the air, high enough to cover his face, a reddened face it was at that.
"Irvin, I said I'm not blind. And people talk, you know. This town isn't as big as you think. The Girls I meet with for lunch at Gallagher's, well, they talk, and word filters back to me. Heck, just yesterday, Maria, our housemaid, found stains, Irvin, *drool stains* on your jacket sleeve. Have you no shame? Have you nothing to say!"
Gladys's hairbrush slammed down hard on the vanity table. There would be a permanent dent in the silver. Domestic tales are often preserved in dents.

Irvin threw the Journal across the king-sized bed. The pages fanned out and gently fell to the bedspread like so much thinly sliced mozzarella cheese bought in Little Italy. Some things of beauty are rarely recognized in the heat of the moment.

"Fine! You see things. You hear things. You know things, I guess. Yes! Yes! I take long lunches at the Tavern or the Rainbow Grill or I end up at Raffles having had too much to drink. So what? A man can't let off steam? I have a stressful job as CEO of Mattress Master. You know that."

Irvin was frustrated. Gladys was at the point of tears.

"But sleeping around, Irvin. Isn't this bed, *our* bed, enough for you?"

With a sigh, a resignation that the jig was up, and now he had to pay the piper, Irvin said, "No, Gladys. No. Okay, it's not. I sleep around. I admit it. I try every bed in my store, hell, in town. I have to. It's my work. It's... it's my passion."

Gladys returned to her brushing. Long... slow... strokes.

To compete, well, she knew her sagging Sealy would never measure up to that. It was just a matter of time before a younger, firmer mattress took hold of her Irvin and enveloped his body. The Girls would talk, and keep on talking, feigning sympathy to her face, beaming bitchy glee to everyone else.

Gladys hated Manhattan. Someday, she would dare to leave this gossipy town, and Irvin, for a man who loved her for her mattress alone. But it takes real money to buy solid silver hairbrushes.

Gladys said no more, climbed into bed and turned her back on Irvin's dalliances.

Unrest, on a well-laid Sealy mattress, shared by two.

Tales from the 2nd Lost Generation

House at the End of the Street

Heading out of Town

By Iva Polansky

With a fresh haircut, his bushy eyebrows neatly trimmed, his nose and ear hair plucked, Eddie was ready for his trip into the wilderness. Eddie was not the outdoorsy type, but he treasured the log cabin he inherited from his uncle. With this ramshackle building deep in the woods, his wildest fantasies had come to life. Heading out of town had acquired a new meaning. Each departure needed careful planning. He liked that. He had several pies in the oven, as he liked to call it, and one of them was ready for consumption. Her name was Monica. According to her pictures, she had velvety brown eyes, curly hair, and a clear complexion.

Monica liked her Facebook friend Petronella. Petronella's mom was in charge of the wardrobe at the Opera House. She would allow her daughter to bring over her new friend to try on the fabulously rich costumes and accessories. Monica was giddy with anticipation as she stood at the Opera House entrance, waiting for Petronella.

"Monica?" The question came from a smiling man. "Yes, it must be you. I'm sorry, sweetheart, but Petronella won't be able to come today. She sent me to tell you. I'm her Dad. That old trouble with her peanut intolerance brought her to the hospital last night, and she is staying in for observation. Her Mom's there with her now. She couldn't text you because her mobile was left behind in the restaurant where the attack happened, and I still have to pick it up."

This was bad news for Monica, and her lips melted into a pout. The man kept smiling.

"Petronella sent me to say she feels sorry. She hopes that you'll meet another time, if you can forgive her."

He patted Monica's shoulder, his smile waning before it brightened again with an idea.

"Unless, of course, you'd like to meet her in the hospital. Wouldn't that be a lovely surprise? She could use a pick-me-up right now. Come, I'll take you to her and we'll buy a bouquet on the way."

Eddie felt the familiar exhilaration as the girl walked by his side headed toward his SUV. He opened the door on the passenger side and she climbed in. He got seated himself and was reaching for the seatbelt when, from behind, his throat got locked in an elbow grip.

"Monica, get out of here this minute," a male voice said. "Mom's waiting for you in the car down the street. Go home and stay there. Now!"

The girl absorbed the shock for a couple of seconds before she sheepishly slipped out of the car.

"You've been stalking the daughter of a government security agent, you jerk," the voice said. "I have a file on you. As of now, the police are digging for bodies around your cabin and, officially, you're on the run. Except you won't be doing any running because I won't have garbage like you alive."

Abruptly, the pressure on Eddie's throat increased. His chin was seized from below, turned to the side and up with a loud snap. At the end of his last ride out of town, Eddie and his SUV went for a swim in a lake not far from his cabin.

The House at the End of the Street

By B.J. Thompson

"Joey, I'm afraid it's your turn, son," said Mr. Durn, a regretful but resigned look on the man as if he himself had ordered this young boy to his own death.

Joey looked up from his Superman comic, glanced at Stephen and Roy seated next to him, rose, and quick replaced his own look of fright with that of steely eyed determination, knowing that what he was about to do had to be done.

"What's the address, Mr. Durn?" asked Joey, straightening his cap and adjusting his tie.

"154 Calley, son."

Stephen whispered to Roy, "Oh, God in Heaven, that's the house at the end of the street."

All four lowered their gaze to the floor, each alone in his thoughts as Mr. Durn offered up the Lord's Prayer and the boys removed their caps.

"God's speed, Joey," Stephen offered, as he and Roy and Mr. Durn followed Joey out the front door of the office, watching the boy slowly bike away, the all-important document tucked safely into his pouch.

It took no time at all to reach Calley Street, for Hidden Valley wasn't a big town, and as he peddled closer to that Victorian beauty at the end of the street, the sunset's amber glow softened the look of the stark white clapboard siding and made the three gold star banner in the window oddly dance.

Joey pushed hard within himself to catch and hold his professional stance. This was no time to soften. He was a boy doing a man's job because all the men in town were in for the fight of their lives. Even boys can have sacred tasks.

Resting his bike against the picket fence, Joey took one last look down the street; and although he had made little noise on his approach, every man, woman and child in the homes on both sides of Calley stood on their porches or out on the street—women holding handkerchiefs to their breast, elderly men removing their hats, children blankly staring. No words, no shuffling, no noise at all came from that growing crowd, yet Death's breath billowed in the air.

Joey filled his lungs, once more realigned his cap and tie, and proceeded up the walk. He rapped three times on the screen door and waited.

Within three minutes, the deed was done and Joey's pouch sat empty. As he biked away from 154, the dying sunlight caught and shimmered a fourth gold star in the window of that house at the end of the street.

Never again would there be a War Department telegram addressed to 154 Calley.

House at the End of the Lane

By Rob Richards

Object Designation #: Hou-4836
Hazard Class: Class D Memetic and Transmogrification hazard (Upgrade to C class pending)
Containment Status: Contained. Requires constant surveillance.

Containment Procedures: The Bureau purchased the houses on either side and opposite Hou-4836, which have been designated as Site 54 and are to be used for surveillance of Hou-4836 and the surrounding streets. An electrified chain-link fence has been erected around Hou-4836 to discourage entry by civilians. Site 54 staff are to conduct 24-hour surveillance on Hou-4836 and use whatever (preferably non-lethal) means necessary to prevent civilian entry.

Following Incident 4836-001 (see Addendum 2), no further entry to Hou-4836 by any personnel during its active phase will be authorized.

Description: Hou-4836 is a two-story rusticated gray-stone located in [Redacted]. The exact age or origin of Hou-4836 has yet to be determined, as no record of its construction or original inhabitants has been found. Local residents all claim that Hou-4836 has been in the neighbourhood for as long as they can remember. Hou-4836 came to the attention of the Bureau as part of an investigation into several seemingly anomalous disappearances in [Redacted].

During its dormant state, the interior of Hou-4836 appears dilapidated and shows signs of being uninhabited for a significant length of time. Near the kitchen, at the rear of the house, there is a door presumably leading to the basement which has been nailed shut. All attempts to breach this door, up to and including the use of high-yield explosives, have failed.

Once every twenty-two days between the hours of 12:00 - 02:00, Hou-4836 enters its active state. Lights appear in the windows and various humanoid figures (hereinafter designated as instances of Hou-4836-01) appear in the house and have what appears to be a dinner party. Initial *exploration attempts (see Addendum 1) have determined that the door at the rear of the house is open at this time. Anyone entering Hou-4836 during its active phase is greeted by an instance of Hou-4836-01 and invited to join the party as a guest. Guests attempting to leave Hou-4836 are forcibly restrained by one or more instances of Hou-4836-01 and [Data Expunged]. Once Hou-4836's active phase has ended, guests ~~are never seen again~~ are trapped behind the basement door and converted via an unknown process into instances of Hou-4836-01 (see Addendum 1).*

~~Hou-4836-01 instances are aware of the outside world but appear unwilling or unable to leave the house.~~ Following Incident 4836-001, Hou-4836 is to be monitored during both of its phases. Any instances of Hou-4836-01 attempting to leave Hou-4836 are to be terminated with extreme prejudice.

13 Deville Way

L. L. Sheppard

Everyone who was anyone in Mrs. Bolgeski's third grade class knew that 13 Deville Way was haunted.

"No way I'm gonna sleep in that place tonight," said Danny, "not even if she pays me a dollar!"

Les piped up, "Me either. No way, no how." He folded him arms.

"Maybe she's one of the ghosts," Kevin reasoned. "I'm not going in there, no matter how nice she seems. It's probably a trap."

Izzy, a quiet bookworm of a girl, softly spoke, "Give her a chance. She's new and my mom says we should be nice to new kids. She already gave me permission so I'm going to the sleep over. Don't be chicken."

The boys all thought about this for a minute and agreed her mom was probably right, and besides, they already had their stuff with them. Their parents, eagerly wanting a night off, had sent each child to school with an overnight bag in hand when they'd heard about the slumber party. It was Kevin who spoke up first, "Fine, who's with me?"

"I dunno...," said Les, usually the bravest kid in their class. He swallowed hard, "If she's a gh-ghost, I don't want none of it!"

"I'll go," Danny agreed with Kevin and Izzy. "Only one way to find out if it's really haunted."

Les, not wanting to ruin his tough-guy reputation, finally gave in, "Okay, but we go together and one ghost shows up, we're all outta there."

They all thought those were reasonable terms and planned to meet after school, one block away from the house at the end of the street.

~~~

At precisely 3:45pm, they gathered.

"Okay," said Les, "we go in, but if anything happens, we run."

They all nodded then crept up the sidewalk, eyes glued on the ominous building. Danny led the way, followed close by Kevin, with Izzy and Les bringing up the rear. Les's
~~~

hand gripped Izzy's elbow, and she rolled her eyes. He shrugged, but didn't let go. 13 Deville Way loomed large and dark as the pack ascended the old wooden porch. Dark grey paint flaked off the siding and a large spider web hung beside the doorbell.

"I don't know about this," Les's voice quivered.

Izzy looked back at her friends, then pressed the ancient bell. The heavy old door creaked open and one eye peered out. A deep voice inquired, "Who goes there?"

The children shifted closer and huddled together, eyes wide.

"We're here for the sleepover," squeaked Danny.

"Yeah, to see Belladonna," said Kevin.

"Come in," the voice enticed.

The door swung wide. All four children peered into the gloomy room beyond but the man had vanished.

"Where'd he go?" asked Les.

"Let's find out," Izzy whispered, and she stepped over the threshold.

The three boys moved in as one lump of arms and feet through the darkened doorway.

The door slammed shut.

Whirling around, the group screamed in unison as a white blob moved towards them. They retreated but slammed into long legs. Heads whipping around, they saw the man towering over them.

They were trapped.

A giggle spilled out of the white apparition and their heads swiveled back, bug-eyed. The giggle grew into a laugh. The form shifted and a little girl's head emerged from under the sheet.

"It's me, sillies," the girl laughed.

"And I'm Belladonna's dad," the man laughed behind them.

"Everyone is scared of this house, so I thought I'd play a trick," Belladonna said, removing the sheet.

The group stood in stunned silence for a few beats then broke into raucous chatter about how great she had fooled them.

"Who wants lemonade," her dad sung, as he walked into the kitchen.

"Me" they all cried, laughing and slapping Belladonna on the back as they followed.

~~~

Ivan peered through the slats of his tomb at the mischievous happenings. Decades had passed since his tiny body had been encased in the walls of the house, and now as a ghoul, it was dreadfully boring not having any children to terrorize. New playmates were hard to come by, but Belladonna had made good on her promise. Delighted, he sealed the exits with an exuberant flick of his wrist and floated into the basement to await nightfall.
~~~

Send a Desperate Plea via a Message in a Bottle

The Winner

By Robert Richards

Congratulations, Customer #1108670476238853!

You've found a Soylent™ Soda Talking Bottle! Soylent™ Soda: Power Fisting your thirst since 2032!

Using our patent-pending technology, we've inserted a message in this bottle congratulating you on winning our Talking Bottle Contest!

Here are the details on how to collect your prize:

Sorry to burst your bubble, but you haven't won jack shit with this bottle. I'm posing as a worker on the Soylent Soda assembly line and am using this talking bottle to get a message out. Sweet deep fried Korean Jesus on a stick; I hope this finds the right person.

My name is Nic Blakey, and I've spent the last three months trying to track down a friend of mine, Brian Yee. The Soylent Soda factory is where the search has led me and let's say there's more than artificial colour and sweetener going into this soda.

The government has been purging dissidents, political rivals and other troublemakers for over a year now. You probably haven't heard anything about this, as for the last decade, ever since the last election, they've been tightening their choke-hold on the mainstream media. Those people aren't clogging up our prison system. They're being sent here, and not as workers.

Shit! Somebody is coming!

Look, I gotta go. Listen, I'm not asking you to stick your neck out for me or my buddy, but I need you to deliver a message for me, or shit is going to hit the fan.

Tell Zouravlioff, "Eagles March Compressed." She'll know what it means.

Thanks, pal. Good luck, and I pray to whatever eldritch forces that govern the cosmos that you're a decent human being.

Message in a Bottle

By L.L. Sheppard

This was the most important task I was ever asked to undertake, and I jumped at the chance to prove my worth. It was a last ditch effort at survival.

I hadn't always been on this island.

The fishing crew I'd gone to sea with didn't realize I was missing when they shipped out.

"I'll do it."

She looked at me, blithe to my response. I knew she wasn't truly asking. She'd picked me because there was no one else, and she demanded compliance. It was just as well. Fate works in mysterious ways.

I'd been alone on this forsaken spit of land for such a long time, categorizing every sea creature and piece of flotsam that found its way along the beach. Really, it was just nice to have an actual purpose again, to be needed, to feel important, if even to one person. Honestly, I was ready to leave it all behind.

I watched her use charcoal from a long-forgotten fire to write a note on a dried palm leaf. She folded the leaf in half, rolled it in a tight tube and secured it with a rock. I gasped when she grabbed me by the neck and shoved it deep down.

"This had better work," she muttered.

We clambered up the sandy dunes to a crest where she planted one rough kiss on my cheek.

I tried to steady myself on the undulating sand when free fall was my end. A great splash. I landed in the azure water. A fantastic jolt. Looking back at the shore, I made a silent, solemn promise that I would find help.

Drifting slowly out to sea, to her, I must be the most important bottle in the world.

Message Found in a Coca-Cola Bottle

By Iva Polansky

PLEASE HELP! Read this carefully.

My name is Adam, and I was kidnapped in front of the Big Grange Elementary School when I was 11 years old. My kidnapper's car was a blue minivan. He grabbed me, threw me in the van and pressed a smelly rag over my mouth. I woke up in a sealed basement with a chain around my neck.

I'm still here.

If I'm "good," I get a bottle of Coke and a Kit Kat. I'm always good now.

My kidnapper's name is Ross, although he insists I call him Daddy. He's about 5'6" and he is fat. He wears a dark-red baseball cap with the letters VGH (whatever that means) stitched in white. Says he is a city worker.

I don't know where we are, but there is a railway near this house and the trains pass at 4:47, 6:55, 8:47, 11:15 a.m. and 2:50, 4:15, 6:44, 9:05, and 11:55 p.m.

I was told by Ross that homeless people pick up our empties. If you are such a person, and if you have found this message, please tell the police right away because Ross is thinking about killing me. I'm no longer small and cute. I'm almost as tall as he is. He's already brought in a replacement, but he keeps him in the other room. I know the little boy's there because I hear him crying. I thought of trying to kill Ross before he kills me, but that chain around my neck would keep me here until I died, anyway. And now there's that other boy.

I've sent dozens of messages but none have been found so far. That's because I put the bottles with my notes inside a plastic shopping bag, so Ross doesn't find them first. Still, God can see that things are worse than ever.
Why doesn't he help? Why?

Thank you. Adam McGrath

Message in a Bottle

By Christianne Parrott

She didn't know if her plan would work. She could only hope and pray. She had all the time in the world to plan, but she was limited, oh, so limited. She had very little information, and almost no freedom or opportunity to execute any plan she formulated. She had to be certain that this time she wouldn't be caught.

Her captor promised horrible punishment should she ever try again to escape. Her attempts had always been discovered at one stage or another, and each time the horrific and degrading punishments escalated. She shuddered to think of it. Daily life was bad enough, but when her captor was angry, it was unbearable.

Her new plan was different. She wouldn't try to escape. She hoped for, and feared, rescue. She had been a captive for so long that she no longer knew normal life. When she was very good, and her captor was in a good mood, she would be allowed the use of a salve for a few days. It came in a tiny bottle. She loved that stuff. It smelled so good and soothed her aching muscles. The bottle was almost empty, and the next time she had it, she would be allowed to finish the contents. This plan was almost a year in the making, or what she thought was a year, she couldn't be sure.

~~~

Holding the empty bottle in her hands, her shaky fingers rolled a note inside.

My name is Claire Powell
I am being held captive in this house
Please rescue me

The "ink," she made with remnants of makeup she meticulously saved and then painstakingly applied to a single square of toilet paper. Blood would have spread too easily on the absorbent sheet, making whatever she would write illegible. She had thought of everything. She had acquired the bottle the night before, remembering her captors' sick smile, and what she had to do to earn it made her stomach turn. At that moment, her feelings were mixed; terror, triumph, hope and hopelessness.

It was now or never.
~~~

She mustered her courage, moved toward the barred window, and with a pounding heart and sweat trickling down her back, climbed as high as she could to slip the bottle through the narrow gap. She prayed her captor wouldn't hear the sound. Once in position, she prayed for its discovery, and let the bottle go.

Message in a Bottle

By William Alan Gardner

I considered by options, angry at myself for getting lost and then coming up with such an idiotic idea. Putting a note into a bottle? Sheesh! It's such a cliché but perhaps more useful than screaming into the wind. I think I've been here a long time and I'm desperate for help. At first I liked it on the island but the freedom and pleasure of being alone has its limits and besides, there's no cell reception. As time passes a certain feeling of panic sets in when you start to think that there will be no rescue; that perhaps no one knows you are here, or cares.

When I found that wine bottle on the beach with its cap still intact, well, it seemed like a sign - good thing they use caps instead of corks these days. Only, what to write? The problem is that I don't know where I am. How do you ask for rescue when you're lost? I'll just write a simple note and hope that someone can figure it out.

Help! I need rescue from a desert island in the ocean. Exact location is unknown but evidently in the tropics. It is a few acres in size with a rocky hill in the middle but otherwise treed. Please arrange for a rescue. I'm desperate. The date now is March 2016. My name is Miles Skovich and I went missing from Revelstoke, Canada.

Perhaps whoever finds this note will turn it over to the authorities and they can find a reference to me in missing person files - surely someone in the office reported me missing - and then track me down from there. Perhaps there's a street video showing me being kidnapped. How else could I get here unawares?

I remember a story about a CIA operative who was injected with a drug by a stranger who bumped into him on the street. That operative woke up in a prison cell with no idea where he was or how he got there. In my case I was just walking down the street heading toward Starbucks for an afternoon latté. As I passed the bakery, I looked in to see what they had on display, but the sun's reflection on the glass temporarily blinded me. I had a falling sensation. The next thing I knew, I was standing on a beach with my briefcase and staring at the sun

At first I was mostly upset. My patent leather shoes were getting soaked by the waves and I'd just bought them.

It was warm and so I sat under a palm tree for a while wondering at my fate. It took days for the reality to sink in that I was alone on a tropical island. I did some exploring despite the limp. It reminded me of that movie with Tom Hanks. Even the island looks kind of similar though I haven't managed to make a fire.

The days seem to blur together with little difference except this rising sense of panic. I need someone to help me, but I'm not sure whether it's for rescue, or to help me die, like Chuck Noland tried to do. To quote a line from an old Tim Robbins movie, I need to "... get busy living or get busy dying."

So I finished the note, waded into the surf and hefted the bottle as far out as I could. Now all I can do is hope. My shoes dried out pretty quickly from their initial dunking but now they're getting scuffed and worn as I trudge around the island. Yesterday I was really depressed, but this morning I feel better despite the persistent sore throat. I really miss that Starbucks coffee. I think I'll go looking for some more cocoanuts then take a swim in the surf. This island has a great beach and it's always warm. After I get rescued perhaps I can come back here for a holiday.

~~~
~~~

"We don't know for sure," said the Doctor, holding out his palms face up. "In surgery we were able to clean and suture the wounds and luckily could save his leg. His concussion is something else. He shouldn't have been free climbing alone. He's lucky to be alive really. We don't know how long the coma will last, or if he'll ever wake up."

Floating Along the River Styx at the Luxor Hotel

By B.J. Thompson

June 1995... 28 months prior. Outside Temperature: 105 F. Poolside. Floating on pool chairs, bottles of Corona in drink holders as misters spritz eternal in their vain attempt to cool off the sunbathing guests... and to the east, the fake, black-glass pyramid looms large behind me...

You see me, don't you? If you want to talk with me, down your beer and shove notes inside the bottle, one by one, and I'll shove notes back. This is the only way.

Not believing my eyes, seeing somebody real, floating, laughing, talking, drinking before me, who in two-and-a-half years would be dead, *he* was already breathing death, and I sense the blackness around me. I think I'm grieving for the future passing of the entertainer, Dean Martin, for I often feel a loss not yet materialized. Yet, as it turned out, my mourning wasn't for Dean. It was for him. I nod, guzzle the south-of-the-border amber liquid, grab a hotel pen and mini pad and start writing;

Why? Why did you leave me? Weren't we a good couple?
Couldn't you, like me, see us grow old together?
You going grey. Us golfing, retired. Still travelling.
Kids?

Corking it with a wine bottle stopper I see floating by, I drop the bottled note in the pool water, swish my arms forward so it will land next to *his* chair. He uncorks, unravels, opens, reads, and responds...

I wasn't told I had to go. Sometimes, He does that.
Even if the taking seems unjust.
He takes because He must. He fast rips off the figurative bandage, to save me, to save you... the hurt.
I had to go. But I'm still here, watching over you... waiting.

Again, the writing, rolling, stuffing, corking, sploshing, swooshing, and it comes back to my chair. I do the same, but in reverse. Tears now. Sorrow? No, more... anger? How dare him. Knowing no way out, I take what time we have left and I speak from the heart, for there is nothing more to do...

We had great times here, didn't we? I mean, in the desert. "Lost Wages," and Palm Springs, watching the sun set in a neon-coloured sky as we solved all the world's problems under water misters, drinking cheap wine. We did it right, didn't we? Knowing what we know now. Again, the same pattern, floating hither, dither, from earthly realms into the mists of the Unknown...

We sure did, Barb. I don't regret a thing.
Order another drink and watch the sun set with me... just this one last time.

Pick a Date in History & Describe Scene

Salem, Massachusetts May 10th in the Year of Our Lord, 1692

By L. L. Sheppard

The word guilty still echoed in Bridget's mind eight days later as the guard hauled her out of the three-by-three foot stone jail cell. Her hands were wrenched behind her back and bound tightly with rough-hewn rope that cut into her wrists. The flickering flame from the sconce in the corridor barely reached the cell, its lumens unable to fully penetrate the suffocating darkness.

"I'm innocent," she pleaded into the abyss, but the guard was unsympathetic to her plight. "Where are you taking me?"

"It's time, witch," was all he could be bothered to say.

He pushed her towards the outer cell doors and she stumbled into the wall. "Get out there," he grumbled, shoving her forward. A stone stairway to freedom or death rose in front of her—cold, judging. She and the steps both knew it was the latter that awaited her.

"Move!"

She began the upwards trek.

Hurled outside to the waiting throng of angry townsfolk, the garish daylight blinded her. Squinting, she saw the twisted faces of people she once shared drinks with, lived alongside, grew up near. The din grew louder as she neared, cheers rising with every new assault from the guard.

"Witch!" one man spat at her, and the accusations began to course anew.

Her captor forced Bridget towards a great beast of a horse, wagon in tow. She stumbled a few steps, and the animal flared its nostrils. One final shove landed her hard, face first, into the dusty bed. Another great cheer ripped through the raucous mob. Bloodthirsty and hungry for her death, they called out her sins, the crowd weaving tales of her using witchcraft against them.

Her judge and executioner, Hawthorne, bellowed, "To Proctor's Ledge!"

With a great thrust, the cart pitched forward.
Panic ignited. This was it. She knew in her heart there would be no escape, but still she cried out, "I'm innocent!"

The roaring masses were uncaring, unhearing, unyielding.

"I'm no witch!" Bridget pleaded with anyone who dared make eye contact, but her efforts turned no profit and her terror swam in stunned disbelief.

The slow progress of the wagon bouncing over the uneven road made her no more nauseous than the turmoil inside her gut. She watched the landscape, fearing the journey's end. Trepidation turned to horror as in the distance, she laid eyes upon a tree. A wooden ladder rested against the trunk, and above, dangling from a study branch, a noose. Bridget gulped the dry air, but it did nothing to calm the storm in her mind nor the roiling in her stomach. Cold sweat broke out over her brow. A rivulet slithered down her spine. Her heart sunk into the soles of her feet.

The tree neared.
The wagon rolled to a creaking stop.

The guard hoisted her out, and the crowd cheered. Grabbing a fist full of hair, the guard hauled her halfway up the ladder. He slipped the noose over her head and cinched it around her neck.

Tight. It was too tight! Her bound hands struggled to break free.

Judge Hawthorne stood atop the wagon, close enough that Bridget could smell his fetid breath as he spoke.

"Bridget Bishop, you have been sentenced to hang until you are dead for the crime of witchcraft and the work of the devil. Do you have any last words?"

Adrenaline surging, Bridget screamed, "This is ludicrous, I'm no witch! I'm innocent!"

She looked at Judge Hawthorne and the people of Salem, tears streaming down her dirty cheeks as she implored them to listen, "Please, I'm innocent. You know me. You all know me. Why are you doing this? What is wrong with you? I'm innocent!"

"Enough," bellowed Hawthorne, "your fate is sealed."

With a mighty blow from the judge's boot, the ladder crashed to the ground, and though the drop was only three feet, it seemed an eternity until the rope reached its end, wringing her neck. Bridget swung from the branch, mouth a gape, desperate to inhale, eyes bulging, lungs burning, legs kicking out for purchase, finding none. Her vision slowly faded from the joyous crowd and ended at the black nothingness of death.

The Day They Shot President Reagan

By Iva Polansky

Zindzi Dalindyebo's restaurant served a budget-oriented Karoo cuisine. On the day in question, the menu featured lamb tails with roasted quince. If you happened not to fancy lamb tails, you could get a hamburger of sorts. Wise locals always avoided the hamburger option. Most locals did not come for the food anyway. They would open a can of beer and enjoy the main attraction of the establishment: the first colour television in Soweto. The technology had not yet reached perfection and since no one—except for the owner's son, Anicet—was allowed to fumble with the TV set, the audience had to suffer the sight of yellow faces and purple lips.

Anicet was gone and no one knew where.

Zindzi pretended not to know either, but people were not buying that. She was too calm for a mother, whose son had gone missing for a week. Besides, Anicet was not a youth with a lust for adventure. He was a choir boy at the local church. Zindzi was not lucky in her motherhood, that much was known. Her eldest son was shot dead in the 1976 student uprising. Then it became a public knowledge that daughter Ina-Cherie was a lesbian. It was decided by some well-meaning men that a good beating and a gang rape would set her right. This therapeutic endeavour had contrary consequences. Once released from the hospital, Ina-Cherie rummaged in her mother's kitchen drawer for the sharpest knife and went after the perpetrators. She finished off one of them, left the second one bleeding from a stomach wound, and the three others had gone into hiding until the police arrested her. She was now serving time.

As for Zindzi's husband, he was remembered as a mild man with an inclination for depression. He was last seen on his way to Jo'burg with the intention of buying spare parts for his bicycle repair shop. He was carrying a relatively large sum of cash and had never been seen since. Zindzi left her job as a maid with a white family and transformed her missing husband's bicycle shed into a restaurant. She was a frowner by nature and no one remembered her smiling. Given her family history, no one expected her to smile any time soon.

On the lamb tails' day, everything went as usual until shortly before seven o'clock in the evening, when the regulars noticed an unprecedented influx of guests, all of them women. Eugene Masango recognized his wife and quickly looked the other way. Out of shyness, or because there were not enough chairs, most women remained standing by the wall.

"What the hell....? All that's missing is the pastor," Eugene murmured to no one in particular. He meant it as a joke, but here was the pastor, too, taking the only available seat at his table. Embarrassed, Eugene tightened the grip on his beer can.

In the news, a yellow-faced anchor with purple lips announced that president Reagan had been shot by some guy named Hinckley, all because of a movie actress. At that moment, Zindzi switched the TV to the cultural channel. This was never done before.

"Hey!" Eugene added his voice to the other protesting regulars.

Zindzi gave them a particularly hard look that reminded them she was Ina-Cherie's mother. Subdued, they watched a boring painting exhibition until the picture switched to the Cape Town Cultural Festival for Coloured People. And there was Anicet, singing an opera aria with an awesome tenor voice. All looked at Zindzi, whose face displayed a happy smile.

Saturday, August 9, 1969

By B.J. Thompson

Crystalline, aquiline sky, omnipresent, penetrating heat, a suffocating kind of quiet in Benedict Canyon.

No birds singing, the usually traffic mêlée down on Sunset Boulevard was mysteriously muffled to the point of non-existent, no voices even, no hint of living things...

The lodge-pole pines bent imperceptibly back and forth, the odd soft creak or groan could have been heard... if anyone with working ears were there to hear...

Freshly washed bedsheets, so stark-white they were against the soft moss-green of the front lawn, blades from that grass grabbed by desperate fingers, those bloody fingers now under those sheets in a rigid grip made some eight hours prior.
Bedsheets don't belong on front lawns, do they?

The hum-click of professional photographic cameras, the click-hum of the pool filter, living beings there now but conversing in reverent tones and only to offer orders. Get this job sewn up as fast as possible. No hair on any man's neck was standing down until that goal was achieved.

Heat, Los Angeles heat, was hitting 96 F at high noon in the shade, low 90s inside the ranch house, the small panes of picture window glass softly cracking from the expansion...

Heating, roasting, burning blood, the metallic odour made one wretch, mixing with the rancid vomit on that lovely lawn. What was once dead quiet and still, now bathed in busy men and bile, assaulting the senses.

Evil would have the final word that day, its speech other-worldly, of course. The vibration of wasted souls translated into the low-frequency, incessant buzz of blue-bottle flies, lapping up the rot, the effuse... the sound growing, the auditory menace invading. Hardened officers are haunted to this day.
Body temperatures would not lower as those five wretched corpses lay baking in the California sun.

~~~

49 years later, if you listen really close, the buzzing of blue-bottle's and the screaming of souls in this dreamy
~~~

place, once the home of Beautiful People, can still be felt and heard.

Buzzing in my mind, since, and evermore.

(The Sharon Tate murders in Los Angeles, committed by The Manson Family)

Revolution

By William Alan Gardner

It was 10:04 on September 11, 2049 and everything was fine. Charlie adjusted his seat and stood up to stretch. He knew that sitting too long was bad for his health and concentration. Around him the five monitors glowed, scrolling and dancing with the data as it came in from the various feeds that monitored Sector Echo Twelve. That was his sector and he maintained a certain pride in its low crime rate. Over the past year there had been only one shooting, no robbery or mugging, and almost no drug dealing - the third best record in the metro area.

Standing, he could see over the cubicle wall, one of hundreds in the slightly darkened room.

He thought of it as the cave which seemed appropriate, considering that it took up the entire basement of police HQ. A special constable sat in each identical cubicle, hunched forward with eyes darting from monitor to monitor. Actually, algorithms and alarms did most of the work but even they could miss something. If you wanted to get promoted upstairs or to street duty you needed to maintain a clean sector, and Charlie so wanted to hit the streets. That had been his dream since he joined the force. That was where the real action happened.

Eighteen years ago, after the terror years, the government forced chip implantation with an ID, a GPS, and a heartrate monitor in all its citizens. It sure made crime prevention easier. Charlie took his seat and scanned the monitors. Nothing looked unusual. The job was usually very boring. One of them, the PRmonitor, displayed a map of the sector with small icons– CitIcons to the geeks - to show where each person was located. You could even watch them move about. If they were in a building you could pull up a ThreeD of the structure to pinpoint them. Two other AVmonitors streamed feeds from CCTV cameras that were located on all street corners, and the third, the RBmonitor, was the audio-video feed from a robocopter if he felt the need to launch one. The last one, the TXmonitor, was where text information and alerts happened.

With this setup you could monitor all activity in the sector - in real time. Clicking on a citizen ikon would bring up all the data and a photo for that person. The feeling of power was, at times, overwhelming - a combination of God, voyeur, and enforcer. They called it "owning the sector."

You could tell a lot about a citizen from their location and heartrate, and who they were with. Some of the new cubes even had a full VR setup where the operator wore a headset, but Charlie found that uncomfortably hot and just a little too real.

He was leaning back, scanning the incoming data when a message appeared on the TX monitor. It was a yellow alert from one of the algorithms saying that an unusually large crowd appeared to be converging on the sector. A few seconds later another message flared, this one from the Twitter-tracking app saying that a flash crowd tweet had been detected with an address in his sector. He checked the PR monitor and saw more and more CitIcons appearing at the margins and moving toward a single point.

What the hell!

He slid his chair over to the robocopter station and entered the instruction to launch. He grabbed the joystick and headed the copter toward the convergence point - a small park at the corner of Mayfield and Rushmore. To his left the PR monitor now showed hundreds of moving Citkons. Another message showed up on the TX monitor, red this time, with an audible alarm. He adjusted the AV monitors to show the CCTV feeds from the appropriate corner and could see a few citizens gathering. There wasn't much traffic, just a few vehicles passing through and a delivery van parked by the local grocery market. Four minutes later the intersection was almost full of people and the robocopter was showing more in the side streets, all headed to the same place. Charlie picked up the phone to call the supervisor.

What is going on? Who managed to get this number of people converging on the same spot? And in my sector. Shit.

Charlie was hovering the copter high above the intersection when an unknown force suddenly pitched it over and he maneuvered the joystick to get it stable again. The picture didn't make sense. Bodies were strewn about on the ground. It took him a few moments to realize what was happening - that where the delivery van had been was the center of carnage.

Oh shit, this will not be good for my sector record.

His attention was drawn to the PR monitor where most of the Citkons of people in the park were turning red as their heartrates dropped to zero. He turned to the TX screen and brought up a seldom used program to list recent dead people in the sector along with their next-of-kin. It normally displayed one or two people at a time. This time the list scrolled down and down and he watched it, mesmerized, until his own heart skipped. He stopped the scrolling and stared at his own name in the next-of-kin column.

Miscellany

Made in China

By Iva Polansky

When he saw the egg, Richard raised an eyebrow.

Was it... could it be...?

It sat on the table along with other odds and ends, partly hidden behind a Meissen figurine of a ballet dancer and other usual antique show finds. He reached for the object to examine it. The surface of patterned lilac enamel and gold trellis carried on top an exquisite bouquet of violets composed of carved amethysts and enameled leaves. The egg rested on three curved golden legs growing from the body.

"Where does it come from?" he asked the vendor who looked underage despite his attempt at growing a beard.

The youth shrugged. "I dunno, except that it comes from the stuff of an old Russian woman. She was over one hundred when she died. Dad could tell you more, but he's not here. He'll be back soon though."

As the boy spoke, Richard's pulse accelerated. A Russian woman. Over one hundred years old. The boy had no idea what he was selling. As for Dad, he wasn't needed. Quite the contrary

"How much?"

"Two hundred and fifty dollars," the boy said. "It's a nice piece. Gold-plated, with real amethysts."

As usual, Richard opened his mouth to bargain. That was the ritual, and he couldn't help himself. "Three hundred," said a female voice, and a hand with painted fingernails made a grab for the egg.

Holding tight, Richard stepped back to acknowledge his adversary. Forty-something, stylish, and determined. This woman knew the egg was an exceptional piece.

"Four hundred."

"Listen," the woman said, "whatever you offer, I will top it. I happen to like that piece. Do you understand?"

Richard's blood boiled. *Arrogant bitch.* "Five hundred," he said.

"One thousand. Try to top that."

Richard got out his credit card. "Two thousand."

When he reached ten thousand dollars, the woman gave up and left. Richard was ecstatic. The last Fabergé egg sold for thirty-one million dollars. There were seven of them missing, and this, he was pretty sure, was one of them.

As he was leaving with the egg wrapped in a Safeway plastic bag, the father returned.
"How is it going?" he asked.

"Dad, you won't believe this," the boy said, excited.

Richard could not help but smirk. These people were completely clueless. He didn't hear the boy say in a much lower voice, "Mom was wonderful."

Truth is Militant
The Blame Game

By B.J. Thompson

The Wabasha Gopher

We Dig For the Truth

A print sheet was placed in front of Herbert Greenway, Editor In Chief of the Wabasha Gopher. On it, the Op Ed cartoon scheduled for Page 3. The cartoonist, Pete Weyy, loomed over the old man with a look that a touchdown he had made on this beaut.

A sketch of four men playing poker—a Priest, a Rabbi, an Iman and a Monk. Above the table, adorning the wall, sat the iconic velvet picture of dogs playing poker, only the dogs' heads were of Jesus, Mohamed, Moses, Elvis Presley and Michael Jackson, all considered 'prophets' in their own time.

A tiny, empty, dusty, picture frame labelled "God" is seen shoved down on the bottom of a bookshelf, buried under great big books entitled, The Art of the Deal by Donald Trump, The Art of War by Sun Tzu, and The Joy of Sex by Alex Comfort.

"Are you nuts, Pete? We can't run this. Remember what happened to that Danish newspaper some years back and then the bombing of that rag in Paris? What, you have a death wish for us or something?"

"Aw, c'mon, Boss, it's not sniping any specific organized religion, it's sniping them all. My take is it's organized religion which is at the core of all of history's greatest conflicts, our conflicts today, and that to fight in His Name is a laugh, showing the ridiculousness of man's take on God. All I'm doing is holding up a mirror, telling it like it is. The Gopher digs for The Truth, remember?"

With his head down, nodding in agreement, Herb let the cartoon run for the 6pm edition.

CNN BREAKING NEWS:

The Illinois town of Wabasha was hit with a reality check today, when an explosion rocketed the news agency, The Gopher. The attack decimated the historic red brick building, instantly killing the Editor In Chief and all in-house reporters. An empty grenade shell was found among the rubble, evidence that it was an RPG hit. No faction or group has claimed responsibility. Church attendance State wide has gone up considerably, clerics stating there has been a 20% increase in tithing.

That same evening, a Priest, a Rabbi, an Iman and a Monk got together to play poker. Stakes were higher than usual as the tithing plates which sat to the right of each cleric were heaping with cash. The same iconic velvet picture still hung on the wall, but one of the clergymen accidentally stepped on the empty frame of God. No cleric would accept responsibility for the break [in faith].

Little Red Riding Hood Meets a Moral Patrol

By Iva Polansky

Entering the forest clearing from the deep shade of the tree line, Little Red Riding Hood squinted to reduce the sun's glare. A rustle in the grass and a sudden burst of agitated feathers as a wild pheasant shot into the air startled her briefly. She took the narrow path through a patch of bluebells where bees kept busy. The buzz of the insects and the soft thud of her feet stepping down at regular intervals were the only sounds until the sharp crack of dead branches announced a presence ahead.

At the end of the clearing three men stepped out of the shade and barred the path. They stood there, waiting. The old man in the middle had a scraggly white beard with the ends dyed saffron-yellow. The other two, both acne-addled teens, held wooden canes.

Little Red Riding Hood had seen the trio in town on more than one occasion. She never had to deal with them face to face, but she heard unpleasant things. It never occurred to her that they would patrol the woods. Upon her approach, the old man spoke first.

"Peace be upon you, little girl."

"My hair is covered with a hood so you have no reason to confront me," she answered defensively, "and my Mom says not to speak to strangers."

"Your mother is a wise woman, but not wise enough to lock you up at home. What's a girl like you doing out alone?"

"I'm going to visit my grandmother."

"Are you? And what is it that you carry in your basket?"

Little Red Riding Hood hid the basket behind her back. "Look," she said, "I'm covering my hair properly and I'm going about my business without bothering anyone. Just please let me go."

She moved forward only to be held back by a cane painfully stuck into her shoulder by one of the teenagers. Both boys grinned from ear to ear. The old man frowned.

"Show us what's in the basket, and then you can go," the old man said.

Her voice thinned with fear. "There's only food for my grandmother. Nothing else, I swear."

"Show us the basket."

There was a ham and a bottle of Chianti. Both unclean, both prohibited.

Little Red Riding Hood got five cane strikes for each forbidden item plus ten more for walking without a chaperon. Long after the men were gone, the bees still buzzed among the bluebells and the wild pheasant returned to the forest clearing.

The Rigatoni Mission

By L.L. Sheppard

"Alright men," Captain Royce "Rigs" Rigatoni's voice sounded over the din of the vessel, "we are up next and we're goin' in hot!"

The air conditioning ruffled our flavour ridges as the ladle sailed towards the large bowl sitting empty on the table.

"In T-Minus 30 seconds, that pristine white paradise below will be stained red with our sauce. We are the brave few, the chosen ones. We alone carry the burden, to sacrifice our lives to the most noble of pursuits... feeding the beast," Rigs proclaimed, his words searing courage into our hearts.

I sat erect, inspiration coursing through my tomato-infused veins. This was my calling. Even as a fresh noodle, I had known my one true path, and finally it was my turn to stand tall where my pasta predecessors stood.

Head up, chest out, I gleefully smiled. Elation surged through every millimeter of my hollow core. My heart felt light, my body, weightless. Euphoria. This was it!

Rigs yelled, "Get ready, men!"

The free fall was exhilarating, but short lived. I landed hard on top of a few other guys. They complained, but the beast was watching, hungry, so I didn't dare move.

The promise land was one bite away, and I was overjoyed.

The beast reached its chubby fingers into the bowl... so close... I could barely contain my rapture, but he snatched my neighbour instead. I saluted him, and his smile beamed out peace and joy.

The great lips closed around him, and finally, he was home. The mouth opened again to chew and the soldier's screams of terror and pain reverberated into my soul.

"No. God no!" his stricken voice shrieked.
The mouth closed again... silence... then opened anew.

"Ah! Please, someone, help m–"

The mouth again shut.

His final death rattle tore through me. I hadn't known it was painful, but then again, no one had ever returned to tell the horrific tale.

Sauce-caked fingers grabbed me and I was airborne.

Oh my God, No! "Someone help!"

Pain shredded every nerve-ending as I was mashed and brutalized by two sharp teeth. The mouth closed, and it was dark. I was alone in my suffering.

Light spilled in, bringing fresh pain as the teeth released me for a moment before mashing down again.

A female voice, "Billy, hunny-boo, don't chew with your mouth open, sweetie. Is the rigatoni good? Yeah, good boy, eat up, then you can go play."

Fade to black.

Into the Woods

By Mel Garland

"This isn't fucking funny anymore!" bellowed the stocky man, frantic eyes darting about in the inky blackness of the dense forest surrounding him. There was nothing. No light source, no sounds of night critters, not even a breeze. It was as though the area was holding its breath, fearful of something dwelling in the woods. He prayed that it was just his sister messing with him like she always did. She knew that despite his tough appearance, he couldn't handle scary things, but with each passing second, his hope faded like a dying candle in a hurricane. Snap! He spun around with such force that he lost his balance, slamming into a nearby pine tree. Steadying himself, he looked in the direction of the sound.

"Katie?" he asked in a hushed voice, straining his eyes against the thick void.

With bated breath, he stood there for what felt like an agonizing eternity, waiting for what he hoped would be

Katie jumping out with a scream, followed by a fit of laughter with her hands clapping in delight at his fright. Instead, what he saw sent him barrelling through the woods at top speed, indifferent to the branches clawing at his skin and clothes. He wasn't grabbed or pushed, nor did he hear anything uncanny. He made out a shape mere feet in front of him. Through laser-focused eyes, he noticed a barely visible image hiding behind a large tree, save for its long fingers curling around the trunk. Just as he decided to call out to his sister and tell her he could see her and to knock it off, he heard someone calling his name from behind, some distance away.

The voice belonged to Katie.

Looking back at the tree, he saw the unnaturally long fingers slowly recede behind the trunk, disappearing as though they had never been. He bolted in the opposite direction and raced towards his sister's voice. He was certain that he would run into Katie and the two of them would high-tail it out of there, but his fear and panic accelerated as time stretched, and his lungs began to burn. He slowed his pace to scan the area for any sign of his sister, but there was none. *Shit!* He desperately wanted to call out to her or use some kind of light source, but he was too terrified of giving away his position to whatever was out there. Besides, the only available light would have come from his phone, which was dead, of course. The original plan had been to head back before dark, but he had lost sight of Katie and lost track of time looking for her. Before he knew it, night had descended.

At this point, he used his hands to feel around in the dark, trying not to trip on any tree roots or logs. His hands came in contact with cold, rough tree bark and he decided to stop for a moment to calm his pounding heart.

Squeezing his eyes shut, he strained to hear anything that might give him a clue to Katie's whereabouts. She couldn't be far. Her calls were in this direction. He wondered if she had seen the same thing and was hiding somewhere nearby. He might be a pansy, but there was no way he was going to leave his sister behind. Come hell or high water, he was determined to find her and get out of there.

As he was planning his next move, his heart caught in his throat. Something began to move slowly underneath his fingers. He screamed, then the wailing stopped mid-stream. All that followed was a deathly silence in the woods.

The End of the Edmund Fitzgerald

By B. J. Thompson

Roaring, rushing, rage-filled noise... a freight train,
Atomic Force... blew out my lungs, flattened my body,
ratcheted me to the back wall,
White... a frothy white-out, suffocating, I am panicking.

Bubbles, blinding... my head hits the ceiling of the wheel-
house, going down...
Oh, my god, we're all going down...

The audible rage dies, the storm remains top-side, quiet
ignites upon descending... True you, oh deathly silence,
Pressure, unbearable pressure, my ears pop, my eyes
bulge,

Alone, others elsewhere, no matter... we're all wrapped in
the frigid papoose of the moody madam Superior,

Down,
Down,
Down.

The storm's fight finished, it's our loss,
Rests still the old girl on the murky floor,
I try holding my breath, but the pressure breaks through.

Lungs void now, eyes popping,
Oh, the pain, the firestorm of pain, water killing me like a flame,

Black,
Unconscious,
No more me–fight, No more me–life.
No more me–nothing... but for you to view?

My corpse floats in that wheel-house to this day, buffed to and fro, wall to wall, suspended in liquid ice, I shall remain.

Still seen by the occasional scuba diver, floating horizontal I am in Superior's arms, my body positioned as if in endless free-fall.
Fingers, face–purple and black, once bloated, now cold,
Eyes dead, staring,
Searching for answers–Why?

Preserved in panic, we 29 men are,
An unending supply of fodder for this great and gargantuan lake.

Author Biographies

CWM

William Alan Gardner

Life seldom follows a straight path. It meanders like a restless rippling stream, flowing over and around obstacles and bouncing with a splash off rocky shores. Where it may lead is, more often than not, a mystery.

William's early life was in a small northern Ontario town that tumbled down a slope between a large lake and a larger forest.

He has always been the observer and chronicler. His special interests are in the areas of culture, economics and history. In these places, one finds fertile ground to grow stories about the human condition and the fundamental drivers of individual action and societal change. He has lived and worked across Canada and travelled extensively around the world. He currently lives with his wife in Calgary.

Mel Garland

Was born in Didsbury, Alberta. This Aquarius was raised by her single working mother alongside her three other siblings. She had a strong interest in art and music from an early age, winning various awards for her works, and appeared on a compilation CD, "Alberta's Finest" in 2002.

Following her mother's death, she moved to Tokyo, Japan where she taught English. She returned to Canada and graduated from Mount Royal University in 2016 with a degree in Sociology and a minor in Religious Studies. She is a supporter of Amnesty International and volunteers for the Calgary Expo.

Her interests include astrology, astronomy, writing, drawing, singing, and reading horror, western comics, folklore and manga—Japanese comics. She currently resides in Calgary where she spends her free time writing, camping, learning other languages, and working on her art.

Christianne Parrott

Is a native Albertan who has always had a great love of books and good stories.

Inspired by her father who would make up his own fantastic tales and fables, and her mother who, under duress, read her bedtime stories far past the age when she could read them herself. She recently began to pursue writing for children and infants.

She enjoys horseback-riding, walking in nature and getting together with her Montparnassian family.

Iva Polansky

A native of Prague, Iva has lived in several French-speaking countries before moving to Calgary.

She has published non-fiction books in the UK, French Canada and, most recently, the US.

Her historical novel, Fame and Infamy, is set in 1870's Paris. The latest of her books, the biographic novella, The War of the Tolstoys, is a dramatic account of the eventful last year of Leo Tolstoy's life. Both titles are available in print and eBook edition at amazon.com.

Robert Richards

Hails from the golden wasteland known as Saskatchewan.

Robert's interest in the macabre was originally sparked by his mother when she told him a bedtime story about a magical bunny rabbit that loved to feast on human flesh.

He lives in a house.

L. L. Sheppard

Loves to tell a variety of stories ranging from erotica to horror.

She loves animals, great and small, but especially her diabetic wiener dog, epileptic German Sheppard, three-legged Pirate cat with one floppy ear, and her ghost weasel.

When not at her day job as a purveyor of ladies lingerie, L. L. is a cheeseburger connoisseur, gamer, and resident mermicorn—half unicorn, half mermaid.

Fascinated by all things creepy and macabre, she is a collector of odd books and strange curios that inspire the tales that bounce around in her imagination.

B. J. Thompson

B. J. grew up in the Lake Country District of southern Ontario, raised very Anglo-Saxon, Northern Irish.

She is a retired public relations liaison and currently a Calgary-based freelance editor and author of literary/historical novels that she lives to pen on either side of Cocktail Hour.

The overriding theme in her works concerns the process of death—death of an icon, an ideal or an event—her works cover those final moments when ultimate truth plays the only role.

B. J.'s books are available at Amazon.com
No More Blood - Epilogue on the Life of Truman Capote & In Cold Blood
Eighteen Minutes to the Beast - a Nixon Watergate Thriller
Sessions - Predator vs. Shrink - Who will survive?

81401215R00135

Made in the USA
Middletown, DE
24 July 2018